Secrets Carved in Blood

Walter Moon

Published by Walter Moon, 2024.

This is a work of fiction. Similarities to real people, places, or events are entirely coincidental.

SECRETS CARVED IN BLOOD

First edition. November 20, 2024.

Copyright © 2024 Walter Moon.

ISBN: 979-8230697374

Written by Walter Moon.

Also by Walter Moon

The Clock's Secret: Every Tick Tells a Tale
Where Secrets Sculpt the Wind: A Psychological Thriller
Flesh and Fractures: The Soul's Descent into Darkness
Beyond the Scream: She's Crying for Help
The Silent Divide: A Chasm of Secrets and Betrayal
The Haunted Frequency: Echoes of the Damned
The Phantom Agenda: The Curse Behind the Truths
When Identities Collide: The Haunted Doppelganger
Lullabies of the Wicked: The Witching Child
Midnight in the Forest: The Girl Who Bewitched
Sorrows of the Moonlit Witch
The Girl With The Twisted Spellbook
Sketches of a Nightmare: A Witch Girl's Grimoire
Fragments of a Killer
Secrets Carved in Blood

Secrets Carved in Blood

Contents:-

CHAPTER 1: THE FIRST Cut
A chilling murder shakes the quiet town, revealing secrets that lie beneath the surface.

Chapter 2: Whispers in the Dark
Detective Mia Hart investigates the crime, uncovering a web of deceit among the locals.

Chapter 3: Unraveling Threads
Mia delves into the victim's past, discovering connections to a notorious cult.

Chapter 4: The Cult of Shadows
As Mia learns about the cult, she realizes they possess knowledge of a disturbing ritual.

Chapter 5: Bloodlines
Family ties are revealed that intertwine the detective with the victim in unforeseen ways.

Chapter 6: The Confession
A haunting confession from a mysterious informant sends Mia down a dark path.

Chapter 7: Reflections of the Mind
Mia struggles with her own psyche as the investigation takes a toll on her mental health.

Chapter 8: Threads of Deception
Not everyone in town is who they seem; Mia encounters individuals with hidden agendas.

Chapter 9: Echoes of the Past
Flashbacks reveal pivotal moments in Mia's life that haunt her, linked to the case.

Chapter 10: The Art of Manipulation
The cult leader's psychological games become evident, pushing Mia to her limits.

Chapter 11: Beneath the Surface
Mia uncovers a series of missing persons connected to the cult's rituals.

Chapter 12: The Gathering Storm
Tensions rise in the town as fear spreads; everyone becomes a suspect.

Chapter 13: Breaking Point
Mia faces personal demons while chasing a lead that could crack the case wide open.

Chapter 14: Truth in Blood
A shocking discovery at a crime scene leads to dark family secrets and twisted loyalties.

Chapter 15: The Final Rites
As the investigation intensifies, Mia learns of a coming ritual that could claim more lives.

Chapter 16: Into Darkness
With time running out, Mia infiltrates the cult, risking everything to save potential victims.

Chapter 17: The Revelation
A confrontation reveals the true identity of the cult leader and their sinister motives.

Chapter 18: Redemption's Price

Mia must make a choice between justice and personal salvation in a heart-stopping moment.

Chapter 19: The Last Stand

A climactic showdown between Mia and the cult threatens to leave nothing but chaos.

Chapter 20: Secrets Laid to Rest

In the aftermath, Mia reflects on the cost of truth, forever changed by the bloodshed.

Chapter 1: The First Cut

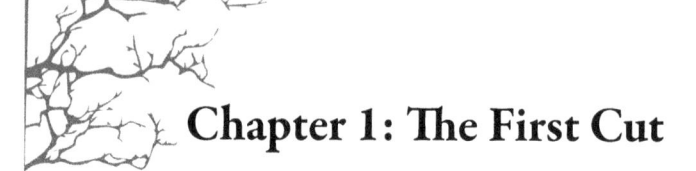

The rain fell in sheets, drumming against the pavement like a thousand restless hearts. In the small town of Ravenwood, such weather was typical—gloomy, oppressive, and often foreboding. But tonight, it felt different. Underneath the steady downpour, there lingered an unsettling stillness, as if the world itself was holding its breath.

Detective Mia Hart sat in her car, the engine idling softly as she stared at the crime scene tape fluttering like ghostly fingers across the entrance to Miller's Park. Flashing blue and red lights illuminated the trees, casting long, eerie shadows that seemed to stretch toward her, beckoning her into the darkness. She could already see the outline of a body being loaded into a coroner's van. The image threatened to cling to her mind, its stark horror uncompromising.

This was her first case back on the force after a year away. A year filled with too many personal scars and unresolved trauma—but she had chosen to return, hoping to reclaim the part of herself that once thrived in the chaos of crime scenes. She gripped the steering wheel tighter, feeling the cold leather bite into her palms. The air was thick with the scent of wet earth and something else—a metallic tang that hinted at the violence that had unfolded here.

"Detective Hart!" A voice interrupted her thoughts, breaking through the haze of rain and memory. Officer Peters, a rookie still trying to find his footing in the world of crime, approached with a grim expression. His uniform was drenched, hair plastered to his forehead.

"What do we have?" Mia asked, forcing her voice to maintain its usual steadiness despite the dread coiling in her stomach.

Peters glanced back at the scene, his eyes reflecting the flicker of flashlight beams cutting through the dark. "Young woman, early twenties. No ID found on her. Just... a lot of blood."

Mia's heartbeat quickened. The absence of identification often spoke to something more sinister—perhaps a hidden life or dark secrets. "Any witnesses?"

"Just a couple of joggers; they heard a scream," Peters replied, sounding almost apologetic. "But they didn't see the attack. They're being interviewed now."

She nodded, turning her focus back to the park, where the trees stood watch like sentinels over the unfolding nightmare. "Let's get inside. I want to see her."

As they approached the perimeter, the air felt charged, a thick blanket of tension wrapped around them. They ducked under the crime scene tape, stepping onto the damp grass that squished beneath their feet. A small crowd of onlookers had gathered across the street, their faces illuminated by the flashing lights, a mixture of curiosity and horror drawn to the chaos.

The victim lay on the ground, her body pale against the vibrant green of the grass, the rain mixing with the blood to create a morbid mosaic. Mia's stomach churned, but she pushed forward. The coroner, a seasoned veteran named Dr. Prior, was already examining the scene, his brow furrowed in concentration.

"Mia, over here," Dr. Prior called, motioning her closer.

Through the chaos, she felt her training kick in—the years of experience honed to read a scene, to understand the story written in the details. She kneelt down beside the body, the rain washing over her, leaving a slick sheen on her skin.

The woman appeared to be adorned in nothing but a white tank top and leggings, the fabric torn and stained. Mia noted the bruising around her neck—fingerprints, deep and angry. Her heart sank. The cause of death would take more time to confirm, but it was clear this was no accident.

"Any signs of sexual assault?" Mia asked, her voice steady, though her mind raced.

"Too early to tell," Dr. Prior replied, carefully examining the girl's face, which held an expression of terror frozen in time. "But I wouldn't rule it out."

Mia felt a chill race down her spine. The shadows around them seemed to close in, whispering secrets just out of reach. "What do we know about her?"

"Just started the search. No ID means we have to get her prints to check for matches." Dr. Prior straightened, glancing back toward the distant lights of the patrol cars. "But I have a feeling this won't be just another murder. There's something... off about it."

Mia's instincts roared to life. She needed to know everything—the victim's story, the circumstances surrounding her death, and most importantly, who had committed such an atrocity. This was only the beginning, but already it felt that their lives were irrevocably intertwined.

Reluctantly, she stood, the rain beginning to lessen as if the heavens were easing their grief for the tragedy below. "Let's get to work. We need to talk to those witnesses and see if we can find any leads."

As she stepped back into the chaos, she couldn't shake the feeling that this murder was only the first cut of many. Each one would carve deeper into the soul of Ravenwood, exposing the darkness that lay beneath its seemingly tranquil surface. This was only the beginning, and she was determined to uncover every secret carved in blood.

Chapter 2: Whispers in the Dark

As the sun rose hesitantly the next morning, filtering through the quilt of gray clouds, Ravenwood appeared deceptively peaceful. The quaint houses, lined with picket fences and adorned with autumn leaves, seemed blissfully unaware of the horror that had unfolded just hours before. But for Detective Mia Hart, the morning felt like a prelude to a storm brewing just out of sight.

Mia sat at her kitchen table, a cold cup of coffee forgotten beside her. She stared at the files spread out before her, the grotesque image of the victim haunting her thoughts. The young woman's face lingered in her mind like a chilling whisper, urging her to dig deeper into the life she had lived before her brutal end.

With a deep breath, she picked up the phone and dialed the precinct. "Peters, I need you to start a background check on our victim. Find out who she was."

"On it, Detective," Peters replied, his voice flavored with excitement but tinged with the unease of his first big case. "I'll also pull any CCTV footage from around Miller's Park."

After hanging up, Mia tapped her fingers on the table, lost in thought. The rain-soaked flakes of memory gathered in her mind—fragments of her own past, echoing warning signs she had often ignored. She shook her head, trying to clear the cobwebs. She couldn't allow herself to get lost in her own darkness. She had a job to do.

Her concentration shattered by a sudden knock on the door. She opened it to find her neighbor, Mrs. Jenkins, a kind but nosy old woman whose penchant for gossip rivaled her love of gardening.

"Mia, dear! Have you heard about that poor girl? Such a tragedy!" Her eyes were wide, shimmering with the thrill of the crime.

"Just a tragic incident, Mrs. Jenkins," Mia replied, forcing a polite smile as she tried to close the door. "I can't discuss it."

"Oh, you know I only want to help!" Mrs. Jenkins pressed through the gap, her wrinkled hands clutching a worn purse. "I heard some whispers last night from the neighbors across the street. They mentioned seeing strange people hanging around the park recently. A group of them, always in dark clothing..."

"Thanks for the information, but I need to follow up on my own leads," Mia said, determined to steer the conversation away.

Mrs. Jenkins frowned slightly but then brightened. "Well, if you change your mind, you know where to find me. I always have my ear to the ground."

As Mia closed the door, she felt the weight of Mrs. Jenkins' intrusive curiosity linger. People loved to speculate, and the rumors could either help or hinder her investigation. She would keep her ears open, but she wouldn't depend on idle gossip.

Within the hour, she arrived at the precinct, the air thick with the smell of stale coffee and urgency. Officers bustled around, each absorbed in their own investigations. Peters was at his desk, brows furrowed in concentration, with a stack of papers strewn around him.

"Got her name," he called out as Mia approached. "Rebecca Lane. Twenty-two years old. Just moved to Ravenwood about six months ago."

Mia's heart sank. A newcomer—a person who may not have established ties here, who might have been carrying secrets that ultimately led to her demise. "What else?"

Peters flipped through the papers. "She was a waitress at the local diner, The Rusty Spoon. No prior criminal record, no known enemies. But there are a few inconsistencies in her social media accounts. It seems she was trying to hide something."

"Let's get to The Rusty Spoon then. We need to talk to her coworkers, see if they noticed anything unusual," Mia ordered, already feeling the urge to uncover the threads of Rebecca's life that had led her to that fateful night.

THE DINER WAS A HUB of morning activity, filled with the sounds of sizzling bacon and clinking dishes. As they stepped inside, the familiar aroma of coffee and grease mixed with an underlying tension that permeated the air. The regular customers, usually jovial, were strangely quiet, their conversations muted as they stole glances at the two detectives.

Mia approached the counter, where a frazzled server, a woman named Kelly who looked about as overwhelmed as a person could get, was filling coffee cups. Her eyes flicked nervously to the detectives. "Are you here about Rebecca?"

Mia couldn't help but nod. "We're trying to understand what happened to her. Can you tell us about her?"

Kelly took a deep breath, glancing around as if making sure no one else was within earshot. "She was really sweet but kept to herself. Never talked about her life much, you know? Just... was always here, working hard. I didn't see her yesterday morning, though. That was odd."

"Did she mention anything—any trouble she was in? Anyone bothering her?" Peters probed, leaning forward on the counter.

Kelly hesitated before responding, her voice barely above a whisper. "There was a guy... I didn't like the way he looked at her. Came in a couple of times, sat in the corner, watching her. He'd leave when she approached for his order. It gave me the creeps."

"Do you remember anything about him?" Mia asked, her instincts firing up.

"He had dark hair, wore a leather jacket. That's about it." Kelly's eyes darted to the door, as if fearing he might step in at any moment.

Mia exchanged a glance with Peters, sensing the importance of this unknown man. "Could you show us where he was sitting?"

The server nodded and led them to a booth tucked away in a dim corner, overlooking the entrance. Mia noted the positioning; it was an ideal spot for someone who wanted to observe without being seen. "Do you remember the last time he came in?"

Kelly shook her head, looking more anxious by the second. "I wish I could help more. It's just... he didn't feel right. I thought I saw him leave just before Rebecca did on that last night. I thought it was strange..."

Mia felt the chill return. "Thank you, Kelly. If you think of anything else, please call us."

As they left the diner, Mia's mind whirled with possibilities. The whispers of the dark clung to her like a shadow, each finding a thread that connected to Rebecca's untimely death. They had a name, a vague description, but it was still a long way from a suspect.

She sensed this was just the beginning; the darkness around this case was only starting to unfurl, revealing hints of something far more menacing lurking beneath the surface of their quiet town. She couldn't shake the feeling that more blood was destined to be spilled, that the whispers were only a prelude to something more insidious.

As nightfall approached, the shadows lengthened, and with each passing moment, Mia felt the weight of secrets waiting to be unearthed—secrets that would carve deeper into Ravenwood's soul, long after she had uncovered the truth.

Chapter 3: Unraveling Threads

Mia sat at her desk, the soft glow of her computer screen illuminating the scattered notes and photographs of Rebecca Lane. Each piece of evidence felt like a thread, delicate yet crucial, in the tapestry of the young woman's life. The more she reviewed, the more questions emerged. Who was Rebecca, and what had compelled her to start anew in a place like Ravenwood?

"Mia," Peters interrupted her thoughts, leaning against the doorframe with a file in his hand. "I think you should see this."

He approached, laying the file on the desk. It was a printout from Rebecca's social media pages, filled with pictures of smiling friends and vacations. But as she flipped through, Mia noticed something unsettling—a stark contrast between the vibrant images of a carefree life and the shadows lurking in the background. There were occasional posts suggesting a darker undertone, cryptic phrases about feeling trapped and needing to escape.

"Did you find out who she was close to?" she asked, flipping through more photos.

Peters nodded, his expression serious. "One of her closest friends was a girl named Lila. They shared a lot of pictures together, and Lila's the one who tagged her when she posted about getting together. I managed to track down her phone number."

Without hesitating, Mia took the lead. "Let's call her. Maybe she knows more about what was happening in Rebecca's life before... before everything."

They stepped into the precinct's interview room, the stark white walls reinforced the gravity of their task. Peters dialed the number and handed the phone to Mia.

"Hello?" a light voice answered, tinged with uncertainty.

"Lila? This is Detective Mia Hart. I'm calling about your friend, Rebecca."

There was a sharp intake of breath on the other end. "Oh no... what happened? Is she okay?"

Mia hesitated, gauging her words carefully. "I'm afraid not. Rebecca was found dead last night."

A heavy silence fell, punctuated only by Lila's muffled sob. "No. No, no... this can't be happening."

"We need to ask you some questions about her," Mia continued, empathy washing over her. "Could you meet us in person?"

"Yes, of course. Where?"

"Meet us at The Rusty Spoon. It's a place she used to work."

An hour later, Lila arrived, her eyes puffy from tears, her hands trembling as she took a seat across from them. Her blonde hair fell in disarray around her shoulders, as if she had rushed out of the house without a thought for her appearance.

"Thank you for coming," Mia said gently. "I know this is difficult."

Lila nodded, tears spilling down her cheeks. "I just can't believe she's gone. We were supposed to meet up last week. Rebecca didn't show, but she always had excuses... I just thought she was busy."

"What do you know about her life here?" Peters asked, leaning slightly forward, eager to grasp any information that could fill the void left by her death. "Did she mention any trouble?"

"No, but... she was acting strange. More withdrawn lately," Lila admitted, wiping her eyes with the edge of her sleeve. "She said she needed some space, but she didn't say why. I thought it was just adjusting to the move, you know? New job, new town."

Mia shared a glance with Peters. "Did she ever mention a guy? Anyone who might have been bothering her?"

Lila's expression shifted as she recalled something. "There was someone. A creepy guy who came in a few times. He'd sit at the bar and look at her like... like she was a piece of meat. I told her to stay away from him. But she wouldn't listen. She thought he was just a lonely customer."

Frustration gnawed at Mia. "What did he look like?"

"Dark hair, scruffy beard... wore a lot of black. She mentioned that he sometimes drove a beat-up old car. I didn't catch the make, but the way she described it made me uneasy. I thought it was just her imagination."

"Have you ever seen him follow her?" Peters pressed.

"I don't know. Maybe." Lila's voice quivered. "Once, I was driving by the park when I saw her talking to a guy who looked like him. But she seemed fine. Smiling."

Mia leaned back, the puzzle pieces starting to reveal a sinister picture. This man—was he just another customer or something more dangerous? "What can you tell us about her past? Did she ever talk about life before Ravenwood?"

Lila hesitated. "She moved here after some... bad stuff happened in her last town. She never wanted to talk about it, but I could tell it weighed on her. She was trying to escape something."

Mia felt a chill seep into her bones. "You don't know what, do you? Any details at all?"

"No, I swear. She was always so careful not to reveal too much."

Frustrated but resolute, Mia looked at Peters, who shared her concern. "Can you think of anyone else she was close to? Anyone who could shed more light on her past?"

Lila shook her head, her face twisted in anguish. "I only met a few of her acquaintances. She didn't bring them into her life here. I thought she was starting fresh. I should have known better."

The sound of her guilt echoed against Mia's heart. Lila was right; there was something buried in Rebecca's history, something that spiraled into darkness and ultimately claimed her life.

"Mia, can we keep her safe?" Peters asked quietly, looking at Lila.

Mia's heart softened for the grieving friend. "Absolutely. We'll make sure you're not alone. If we find anything, we'll keep you updated."

Lila smiled weakly, her expression shifted from despair to determination. "Please, just find who did this to her."

As they stepped out of the diner, the sunlight seemed muted, a stark contrast to the storm brewing inside Mia's mind. Each question spun outward, creating an expanding web of secrecy surrounding the town and Rebecca's life.

Mia instinctively turned her gaze toward the park, imagining the myriad threads that connected its inhabitants, each harboring secrets of their own. She realized that unraveling Rebecca's story would lead her deeper into the murky depths of Ravenwood, where dark desires and turbulent pasts coalesced in whispers.

With resolve brewing in her chest, she decided that she would peel back those layers, no matter how tightly woven they were. The truth was out there, tangled and hidden—but Mia Hart was determined to expose every shadow, every whisper, until the last thread unraveled.

Chapter 4: The Cult of Shadows

The late afternoon sun dipped below the horizon, casting long shadows across the streets of Ravenwood, darkening the very corners that had once seemed so familiar. Mia felt it in the air: an unease that settled in like fog, wrapping around her as she drove toward her next destination. The diner's chatter faded in her mind as she played back Lila's words, each one resonating with a sense of urgency that refused to release its grip.

"Cult," Mia muttered under her breath, thinking of the gossip she had heard from the townsfolk. "It's time to dig deeper."

After a brief detour to gather information at the precinct, she learned about a group that had operated in Ravenwood for decades—The Cult of Shadows. They were whispered about among the locals, a shadowy presence that flitted through the town's history, rumored to indulge in dark rituals that involved manipulation and control.

Mia sat in her car outside what had once been the cult's meeting place, an old abandoned church on the outskirts of town. The Gothic architecture loomed ominously against the twilight sky, its weathered stones and broken stained glass casting eerie patterns on the ground. Vines crept along the walls like fingers grasping at secrets long buried.

As she stepped out, a chill ran through her, amplified by the rustle of leaves and the whisper of the wind. She pulled out her phone and checked the articles she had saved, each detailing past rituals, missing persons, and the cult's enigmatic leader, known only as "The Seer."

There were references to members vanishing, often leaving behind nothing but their echoing laughter, as if they had simply melted into the shadows.

"Stay sharp," Mia reminded herself, taking a deep breath. The air smelled of damp earth and decay, a reminder of the history that lay beneath her feet. She approached the church, careful to avoid the broken glass that littered the path.

Inside, the atmosphere thickened. Dust motes floated in the dim light as Mia's flashlight carved through the darkness. Shadows danced along the walls, seeming to whisper secrets of their own. She scanned the interior, noting the remnants of forgotten gatherings: old pews overturned, dilapidated altar decorations, and sinister markings etched into the wooden beams.

Suddenly, the sound of a creaking floorboard startled her. Heart racing, Mia trained her flashlight toward the source, her breath catching in her throat. "Anyone there?" she called, steadying her voice.

Silence wrapped around her like a shroud, heavy and unyielding. Ignoring the pulse of fear thrumming in her chest, Mia crept deeper into the church, where the air felt charged, almost electric. She stepped carefully through the main hall, her eyes widening as she noticed faded photographs tacked to the walls.

They depicted gatherings, people dressed in dark robes, faces obscured or turned away, an eerie sense of unity binding them. On closer inspection, she recognized some faces—town residents she had seen, now translucent apparitions trapped in time.

Mia's instincts screamed at her. This wasn't just a cult; it was a powerful network. The idea that members of Ravenwood's community might be connected to Rebecca's murder sent a shiver racing down her spine.

Determined to find more, she rummaged through a stack of old papers near the altar. Most were illegible but soon she stumbled upon a crumpled flyer advertising a meeting. "Join us under the moonlight," it read in elegant script, "and uncover the truth that lies within the shadows…"

A noise from the back interrupted her thoughts, the unmistakable sound of a door creaking open. She spun around, flashlight beam slicing through the darkness, heart hammering in her chest. But it was only the wind, coaxing an old door ajar and creating a spectral wail that resonated through the church.

Still, she wasn't alone. The sensation prickled at the nape of her neck, a feeling that eyes were watching her. Focusing her thoughts, she turned to the back room, where the whispers of the past felt strongest.

Mia tiptoed through the narrow hallway, finding herself in a cramped space filled with dusty crates and cobwebs. In the corner, a small, locked box caught her eye—aged and battered. Without thinking, she pulled out her trusty multi-tool, prying it open with trembling hands. Inside, she found journals, their pages yellowed and brittle, some filled with passages that hinted at dark rituals, despair, and a cryptic prophecy: "When blood spills in the name of shadows, rebirth comes from the depths."

As Mia flipped through the journals, her breath quickened. They described initiation rites, sacrifices, and whispers of a coming event—a ritual that was supposed to elevate their members beyond the mortal realm. Panic flared in her gut as she realized that the timing coincided with Rebecca's murder.

"Mia? You in here?" Peters' voice sliced through the tension, pulling her back from the edge of her thoughts.

"Yeah, just… looking around," she called back, hastily stuffing the journals into her bag. She needed to analyze this later, but for now, time was running out. She couldn't risk getting caught alone.

As Peters arrived, he immediately sensed the charged atmosphere. "What did you find?"

"Evidence of a cult operating in Ravenwood. Their rituals, their beliefs... and it looks like they might be connected to Rebecca's death. We have to dig deeper into this."

"Let's clear out of here before anyone else shows up." His eyes darted nervously around the dim light, as if he expected shadowed figures to emerge at any moment.

They exited the church, the night air feeling stifling and heavy. As they drove back into town, Mia couldn't shake the feeling that danger was creeping closer, lurking just beyond the periphery of their investigation. The whispers of the shadows now echoed in her mind, a cacophony of secrets begging to be unearthed.

"Do you think we should go public with this?" Peters asked, glancing at Mia as they turned onto the main road. "People deserve to know."

"Not yet," Mia replied firmly. "We need evidence, something solid enough to force their hand. If the Cult of Shadows is as powerful as it appears, we can't risk stirring the pot until we're ready."

But even as she spoke, the dread that coiled in her stomach twisted tighter. The deeper they delved into the darkness of Ravenwood, the more she feared what they might uncover—and what it might mean for any truth-seeker daring to unravel the threads of the Cult of Shadows.

Chapter 5: Bloodlines

Mia sat at her desk, the weight of the journals from the abandoned church heavy in her bag, each page a reminder of the darkness woven into the fabric of Ravenwood. Each entry had whispered sinister secrets, but it was the cryptic prophecy about blood spilling in the name of shadows that haunted her the most. It felt as if they were running against time, and the shadows were closing in.

Her thoughts were interrupted by Peters, who entered the precinct carrying a stack of files. "I've pulled together everything we have on missing persons in the area that match the time frame of Rebecca's arrival in town," he announced, dropping the files onto her desk with a satisfying thud. "And you won't believe what I found."

"What is it?" Mia asked, leaning forward, her heart beginning to race.

Peters flipped through the papers, his fingers trembling slightly. "There are multiple cases of young women disappearing over the past few years, all with connections to Ravenwood. They have similar profiles: young, new to the area, and all seemingly unconnected until now."

"Do we have names?" Mia focused, scanning the files for anything that would provide greater insight.

"Yeah, here we go." Peters pulled out a sheet and held it up. "Emily Carter, Sarah Bloom, and Rachel Meyers. All last seen in Ravenwood while they were trying to escape their pasts. Each of them was reported missing within months of moving here. All women—just like Rebecca."

"Let me see." Mia took the sheet, her mind whirring. "Did any of them have ties to the cult? Friends? Family?"

"I'll start cross-referencing," Peters promised, jotting down notes. "But I did find one intriguing connection: Sarah Bloom's mother. She was a prominent member of the community before moving away to escape some scandal. I think she might have some information."

"Let's pay her a visit," Mia decided. "We might find answers about her daughter and possibly Rebecca. If the cult's influence has roots in this town's history, we need to trace them back."

AFTER A SHORT DRIVE, they pulled up to the modest home of Carol Bloom, a woman whose face had once graced the local news. The house, slightly worn with age, had a peaceful exterior, but Mia sensed the unease lurking just beneath the surface. Carol had fled Ravenwood, only to find her daughter caught up in its darkest shadows.

Mia and Peters approached the front door and knocked. After a few moments, the door creaked open, revealing a weary woman with tired eyes and graying hair. "Can I help you?" Carol asked, her voice steady yet weary.

"Mrs. Bloom, we're detectives with the Ravenwood Police Department. We're investigating the disappearance of your daughter," Mia said gently.

At the mention of Sarah's name, Carol flinched, her body stiffening. "What do you want to know?"

"We have reason to believe that your daughter's case might be connected to others, possibly including Rebecca Lane," Peters interjected, trying to gauge her reaction. "We'd like to ask you some questions."

Carol's expression hardened, and she hesitated before stepping aside. "Come in."

The interior of the house was filled with an aura of nostalgia, framed photographs of a younger Sarah adorned the walls, her face reflecting joy and hope before the shadows of the past fell upon her. Mia felt a pang of sorrow for the mother, who had lost so much yet was struggling with her own demons.

"Please, sit." Carol gestured to the modest living room, her gaze fixed on the window, as if searching for answers in the fading daylight. "I don't see how I can help you. I've been trying to forget."

"Mrs. Bloom, if there's anything you remember, anything at all that might help us, it could make a difference," Mia urged softly.

Carol took a deep breath, her fingers trembling slightly as she fiddled with a bracelet on her wrist. "Ravenwood has a way of holding onto you... It's as if the very ground is steeped in secrets. Sarah was trying to escape something. She told me she felt like she was always being watched. I thought it was just paranoia."

"Was she involved with anyone? Did she mention a group or any friends?" Peters leaned in, his voice gentle but probing.

"I don't know," Carol murmured, her voice barely a whisper. "She had a few friends but they disappeared too, one after the other. And then one day, she just... vanished."

Mia exchanged a glance with Peters, feeling the weight of Carol's words settle in the pit of her stomach. "Did she ever mention a cult? Anyone by the name of 'The Seer'?"

A flicker of recognition crossed Carol's face. "I've heard the rumors. Dark stories of rituals and gatherings. I thought it was just folklore, something to frighten the children. But after Sarah disappeared, I couldn't shake the feeling that there was something to it. I looked into it..." Her voice faltered, then she continued, "What I found... it scared me. I couldn't bear the thought that my daughter might have been involved."

"What did you find?" Mia pressed, leaning forward.

"Just whispers—stories of a circle that calls themselves the Cult of Shadows. They're all about power and control, using fear as their weapon. I never thought they were real... until my daughter was taken."

Mia felt her heart race. "And you didn't think to report this?"

"I thought it was my grief talking!" Carol exclaimed, eyes wide. "I didn't want to believe that something like that could exist here, in our town! I was scared. I thought I was losing my mind. I thought Sarah would come back."

Peters looked at Mia, understanding dawning in his expression. "Do you have any of her things? Any journals or letters that might give us insight into where she disappeared?"

Carol nodded slowly, steel returning to her spine. "I have a box in the attic. It was never easy to go through it. I'll get it."

As she climbed the stairs, Mia turned to Peters. "We need to find this cult's influence in the past. If they've been operating here for years, we might find more missing persons."

"Agreed. We should also expand our search for connections among the recent disappearances. If they're as organized as I suspect, we need to figure out how to take them down," Peters replied, determination sparking in his eyes.

Carol returned moments later, carrying a weathered box filled with papers, faded photographs, and clothes that smelled faintly of her daughter's perfume. "These were all I could bring myself to keep," she said, placing it on the coffee table with trembling hands.

Mia opened the box, carefully sifting through the contents. As she pulled out a journal, worn and frayed, her heart sank. In Sarah's handwriting, she saw fragments of thoughts describing feelings of entrapment, of being drawn into something dark and powerful. The last entry sent shivers racing down her spine: "I can't escape the shadows anymore. They are calling me back."

"We're going to find what happened to Sarah," Mia promised, looking up to meet Carol's gaze with fierce determination. "And we won't let Rebecca's death be in vain."

As they delved deeper into the secrets of the past, Mia could feel the bloodlines—the ties that bound these women to something much larger than themselves. The threads of fate were woven into the very fabric of Ravenwood, and she was determined to unravel them, no matter how deep the shadows ran.

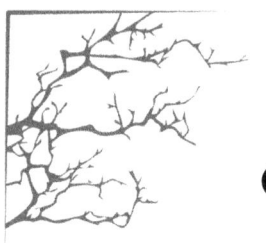

Chapter 6: The Confession

The rain had returned, drumming steadily against the windows of the precinct like a thousand restless fingers. Inside, the atmosphere was a mix of resolve and anxiety as detectives reviewed the findings from the previous days. Mia sat at her desk, paper trails strewn across the surface—notes, photographs, connections that began to interweave and tangle like a dark tapestry.

Her thoughts drifted as she stared blankly at the wall, replaying the latest evidence they gathered from the abandoned church. The journals, with their chilling descriptions of rituals, haunted her. The implications were darker than she had imagined, and yet there was still something nagging at her—a thread that felt unfinished.

"Hey, Mia!" Peters burst into the room, his excitement palpable. "You've got to see this."

She turned sharply, curiosity piqued. "What's up?"

"I tracked down someone connected to the cult. An ex-member who's been keeping a low profile," he explained, barely containing his enthusiasm. "And they're willing to talk."

Mia's pulse quickened. "Where are they?"

"I set up an interview in one of the back rooms. They'll be here in ten minutes."

Every instinct told her that this could be a breakthrough—if this person could provide insights into the inner workings of the Cult of Shadows, it might finally lead them to Rebecca's killer.

Moments later, a thin, nervous figure entered the room—a man in his early thirties with unkempt hair and wide, anxious eyes. He looked around, as if expecting shadows to swallow him whole.

"Thank you for coming," Mia said, motioning him to sit. "I'm Detective Hart, and this is my partner, Detective Peters. We know this might be difficult, but your insights could be crucial to our investigation."

The man swallowed hard, his hands trembling. "My name is Ben. I... I left the cult a few months ago. I'm scared."

"Scared?" Peters pressed gently. "Of what?"

Ben hesitated, glancing at the door again. "The others... they don't take kindly to those who leave. They'll find me."

Mia leaned forward, eyes steady. "Why did you leave, Ben?"

He glanced down at the table, taking a moment to collect himself. "I thought I was joining a community, a safe place. But then I saw things—things that terrified me. Rituals that... that were not just ceremonies. They were blood sacrifices."

A heavy silence enveloped the room as the weight of his words sank in. "You're saying they killed people?" Mia asked, her heart racing.

"Yes. They said it was for power. To appease something... something dark." His voice trembled. "Rebecca Lane was one of the girls they chose. I didn't know her, but they spoke about her. They had plans for her."

"Plans? What kind of plans?" Peters interjected, urgency lacing his tone.

"They wanted to use her in the Harvest Moon ritual—a powerful ceremony. Every year, during that time, they believe they can gain strength by offering a chosen one. She was selected, and they intended to make her their sacrifice."

Mia's mind raced. "And how did you find out about this?"

Ben shifted uncomfortably in his seat. "I was there when they discussed it. They mentioned something about her background... dark dreams or visions. They believed she was special, connected to their rituals. But when I realized what they were doing, I had to get out."

"Did you see who was involved?" Mia pressed. She needed names, connections—anything that would link him to the cult and to Rebecca's death.

"I did. The leader, The Seer, was orchestrating everything. But there's also a small group of loyal followers—ones who do his bidding without question," he whispered, fear dancing in his eyes. "I don't know all their names, but I recognized a few faces. They've lived in Ravenwood for years."

"Ben, this is important," Mia urged. "We need those names, and we need to know the details—anything that will keep you safe and help us find Rebecca's killer."

"I can try," he stammered, eyes darting nervously. "But... you have to protect me. They'll come for me if they find out I spoke to you."

"What can you tell us about The Seer?" Peters pressed, determined to get the information they needed.

"He's charismatic," Ben said, his voice shaking. "He's got followers under his spell. He preys on their insecurities, their need for belonging. If you cross him, you're a target."

"What about Rebecca?" Mia's heart thudded in her chest. "What else did they say about her?"

"They mentioned her past, something about her family—something dark that happened before she came to Ravenwood. They believed it made her a perfect candidate. I didn't understand it all, but I knew it was bad."

Mia exchanged a glance with Peters, urgency flooding her thoughts. They needed to find out what Rebecca had been running from before she had arrived in Ravenwood. "Is there any way you can help us identify the other members?"

Ben nodded hesitantly. "Perhaps. But I'll need to get in touch with some contacts. There are still others who might be willing to talk."

As the conversation drew to a close, Mia felt a mix of hope and trepidation. They had gained a foothold into the dark world of the cult, but it came with increased risk. She leaned forward, her voice steady. "Ben, if you come with us, we can provide protection. You won't be alone. But you need to be honest with us every step of the way."

The weight of the decision pressed on Ben's shoulders. "Okay... I'll do it. I need to make this right."

As they prepared to leave, Mia felt a knot of determination tighten in her chest. They were stepping deeper into the shadows, but they were no longer alone. They had a source—a confession that could unravel the darkness consuming Rebecca's life.

In the days to come, they would have to tread carefully through the underbelly of Ravenwood, confronting the very essence of fear and secrecy. The Cult of Shadows had a talon-like grip on the town, but Mia was resolved to bring light to the darkness, one confession at a time.

Chapter 7: Reflections of the Mind

Mia sat alone in her dimly lit apartment, the hum of the city outside muted by the heavy curtains. Every surface was cluttered with case files, notes, and photographs of Rebecca Lane. The overwhelming evidence of darkness and despair surrounded her, amplifying the unease that had been gnawing at her since the investigation began.

Coffee cups littered the table, remnants of sleepless nights spent poring over details and piecing together fragments of a shattered life. She rubbed her temples, trying to dispel the fog clouding her thoughts. But even in the silence, her mind echoed with the whispers of the past—memories she thought she had buried but now surfaced relentlessly.

Mia had always been one to confront her demons head-on, a trait that served her well as a detective. Yet, lately, the shadows of her own life had begun to intrude on her ability to focus on the task at hand—solving Rebecca's murder.

After a moment, she pushed herself away from the table, pacing the small space. She needed fresh air. Maybe a walk would help clear her mind.

As she stepped outside, the cool evening air wrapped around her like a balm, but it did little to soothe the turmoil within. She wandered aimlessly through the streets of Ravenwood, her thoughts swirling like leaves caught in a gale. Past the diner, where Rebecca had once served coffee with a smile, and toward the park, now cloaked in darkness and foreboding.

The park seemed different at night—almost alive. Shadows shifted among the trees, whispering faint secrets, their rustle echoing eerily against the quiet. She had always loved this place as a child, but now it felt sinister, treacherous. She took a seat on a weathered bench, staring up at the stars partially obscured by drifting clouds.

Then came the memories. Childhood nights spent here with her father, reassuring words woven into the fabric of her youth. He had been her hero, the steady hand guiding her toward a future where she could be anything she aspired to be. But that future had darkened the day he was taken from her.

"Mia... you need to stay strong," her father's voice echoed in her mind. She recalled the warmth of his presence, laughter entwined with a love that felt eternal. If only that were true.

But everything changed when the call came in. A routine traffic stop turned deadly because someone decided to run. A bullet that wasn't meant for him shattered her world, leaving her lost and adrift. No warning, no time to say goodbye. Just emptiness.

"Focus," she whispered to herself, shaking her head as the tears threatened to spill. She couldn't allow herself to be overwhelmed. Rebecca Lane's case was demanding her full attention.

As she sat there, the shadows deepening around her, she recalled the details—Lila's desperation, the dark-eyed stranger in the diner, the meetings of the Cult of Shadows. Each detail played out in her mind like a twisted film, strands connecting in ways she couldn't yet see. Rebecca had been running from something, but what?

Suddenly, the sound of footsteps broke the silence, and Mia's heart raced at the thought of an intruder. She turned to see a figure approaching, but it was only Peters, jogging toward her, his breath visible in the crisp air.

"Mia! I thought I'd find you here," he said, collapsing onto the bench beside her. "You've been working too hard. We need to talk about what we've found."

"Is it about the cult?" she asked, grateful for the distraction as Peters pulled out his phone to display a series of pictures.

"Yeah. I figured we should get a visual on the people Rebecca may have been associated with." He pointed to an image of a gathering in the woods, robed figures encircling a fire. Mia recognized the location from the outskirts of town—an area long associated with the cult.

"Who took these?" she asked, observing the details more closely. The flames cast flickering shadows that seemed to animate the crowd, faces obscured but some identifiable.

"Anonymous tip. Someone was watching them. The pictures were sent with a note that indicated an upcoming ritual. It could be our chance to get evidence."

Mia's pulse quickened. "If there's a ritual, this could lead us straight to The Seer. We have to go."

"Tonight?" he asked, unsure and slightly apprehensive.

"Why wait? They won't expect us," she urged, adrenaline coursing through her. Tonight was the perfect night to find answers, before darkness encroached further and claimed more lives.

As they gathered their things and prepared to leave, Mia could feel her father's presence in her thoughts, a guiding force urging her on. Hope intertwined with determination—for Rebecca, for herself, and for the shadows still looming within.

The car ride was tense but charged with anticipation. Mia's mind danced between memories of the past and the present urgency. She needed to confront the dark remnants of her life, to face the shadows not only of Rebecca's murder but of her own long-buried pain.

As they arrived at the meeting spot, the darkness enveloped them, an echo of the secrets lurking within the town. The flickering flames came into view, silhouetting a gathering that felt otherworldly, each figure a reminder of what she fought against.

Mia and Peters exchanged determined glances, steeling themselves for what lay ahead. There would be no turning back. They were diving deep into the abyss—a realm filled with shadows and whispers where danger thrived, and truths awaited in the dark.

Chapter 8: Threads of Deception

The morning sun bathed Ravenwood in an unsettling warmth, illuminating the fading remnants of the previous night's storm. For Mia, the idyllic setting felt like a cruel irony against the backdrop of a town that held so many hidden truths. Armed with the journals retrieved from the abandoned church, she sat at her desk in the precinct, pouring over the pages, her heart pounding with revelation.

"Hey, Mia." Peters entered, a cup of coffee in hand. "Did you get any sleep?"

"Not much," she admitted, barely glancing up. "This is worse than I thought. The cult—The Cult of Shadows—has been operating right under our noses for years. They're connected to missing persons cases, and it seems they might have conducted rituals in the park."

Peters raised an eyebrow, stepping closer. "Rituals?"

Mia nodded, flipping to a page that detailed a series of occurrences that the cult believed were sacrificial offerings meant to appease dark forces. "Look at this—specific moons and recurring dates suggest they've been trying to summon something."

"Summon what?" Peters asked, leaning over to get a clearer view of the battered pages.

"Something they refer to as 'The Unseen.' It sounds like a way to bolster their power, but it's not just superstition. There's a line here about blood offerings leading to ascension." She shivered, recalling the bloodstains that had once stained Miller's Park.

"We have to get this info to the higher-ups. If they've been involved in all these disappearances..." Peters trailed off, unable to finish the thought.

Before Mia could respond, the heavy thud of footsteps echoed down the hallway. The precinct's chief, Tom Severin, entered the room, his expression grim. "Detectives, I need to speak to you both."

Mia and Peters exchanged glances and straightened in their chairs. "Yes, Chief?" Mia asked.

"I've just received word that we may have a lead on our victim's murder." He placed a folder on the table. "Witness reports indicate that Rebecca Lane was seen having a rather heated discussion with a man just days before her death. Witnesses described him as tall, with dark hair and a leather jacket."

Mia felt her heart race. "That fits the description we got from Kelly and Lila. Did they get a name?"

"Not yet, but we're pursuing it. I want you two to follow up on this today. Talk to anyone who might know her habits, her friends... anyone who might shed light on this man." Chief Severin turned to Peters. "Get the local businesses to see if they have any security footage. We need to know who she was with and when."

"What if this is connected to the cult?" Mia interjected, her eyes narrowing. "They might have a hold on her, or she could have known something about their operations."

"Right now, I want to focus on the immediate lead." Severin's voice was firm. "We can check out your theories later, but this is our best shot at making any progress. Understood?"

Mia felt the fraying threads of urgency tugging at her. "Understood, Chief."

As Severin walked away, she felt a need to act quickly. "Let's head to The Rusty Spoon again," she said to Peters. "If Rebecca was there recently, maybe we can get more information from her coworkers."

AT THE DINER, THE ATMOSPHERE was tense, the usual banter replaced with hushed conversations. As they entered, several patrons glanced up, their eyes clouded with concern. Mia felt the weight of their stares; the recent tragedy lingered in the air like a specter.

"Hey, Kelly," Mia called to the server who had previously shared her unease about the mysterious man. "Got a minute?"

The young woman approached cautiously, wiping her hands on her apron. "What's going on? Is there more news about Rebecca?"

"We're trying to gather more information about her last days," Peters explained. "Did she mention anything about someone following her or maybe having conflicts with customers?"

Kelly hesitated, her brow furrowing in thought. "There was something... a few nights before she disappeared, she seemed really on edge. I noticed her talking to that guy a lot, the one we thought was creepy. But that night, she told him to leave her alone."

"She confronted him?" Mia asked, intrigued.

"Yeah. I was serving another table when I saw it go down. He got right in her face, and she looked scared." Kelly shivered slightly. "She didn't detail it, but it felt serious."

"Do you remember what he said?" Peters pressed.

"Not word for word, but it felt like he was demanding something from her," she recalled, glancing around. "He kept saying something about knowing her true potential, about the 'shadows' claiming what was theirs... It was odd."

Mia exchanged a glance with Peters, the connection sparking with intensity. "Let's go through the footage from the diner, then."

"Right now?" Kelly looked apprehensive. "What if he comes back?"

Mia softened her tone. "We'll be here with you. It's important that we see if we can identify him."

Reluctantly, Kelly agreed, leading them to a back room filled with old monitors and recording devices. As they reviewed the footage, tension hung like smoke in the air, thick with anticipation.

They scrolled through various recordings of the diner, fast-forwarding through hours of mundane activity until they arrived at a night just days before Rebecca's death.

"There! There she is!" Peters pointed at the screen as a figure came into view. A woman—Rebecca—sat at the bar, her eyes cast down. Then the familiar man with dark hair and the leather jacket entered the frame, taking a seat two down from her. He leaned in closer, his gestures animated yet menacing.

"Can you pause it?" Mia ordered as he started to engage with Rebecca, their conversation almost muted by the din of the diner.

Suddenly, Rebecca's body language shifted. The tension in her shoulders, the pained expression on her face as she seemed to plead with him. Mia leaned closer to the screen. "What was he saying?"

"Just wait," Peters whispered, eyes fixed on the developing scene.

As they watched, the man leaned in, his mouth moving with fervor. Rebecca shook her head, her expression turning from confusion to outright fear. Then, with a determined stance, she stood up and faced him. The expression of a woman who had finally had enough.

"He's getting aggressive," Peters murmured, a hint of disappointment in his voice.

Through the static and the distant sounds of laughter, they caught snippets of the confrontation. "You don't understand, do you?" the man said, his voice low and threatening. "They won't let you go. You're one of us, Rebecca. You can't escape the shadows!"

"That's it! We need to figure out who he is!" Mia demanded, her heart racing.

Peters zoomed in on the man's face, determination etched across his features. "This guy isn't just a customer; he's part of something sinister. If he's linked to the cult..."

"Let's see if we can identify him with the images we have." Mia felt the threads of deception starting to weave themselves into a sinister pattern. This was more than a murder; it was a struggle against a force that had long been hidden beneath the facade of their town.

Fueled by urgency, they decided to head to the precinct to see if they could match the man's face with known criminal databases or any prior cult sightings.

As they stepped out of the diner, one thought clung to Mia's mind: the more they uncovered, the clearer it became that Rebecca's death was not just an isolated act of violence. It was a thread pulled tight, connecting them to a much darker reality lurking just beneath Ravenwood's surface—one that promised to entangle them all in its web of deception.

Chapter 9: Echoes of the Past

The morning light filtered through Mia's window, illuminating the scattered remnants of her chaotic investigation. Her kitchen table was cluttered with photographs of Rebecca, notes about the Cult of Shadows, and pages from the journals she had found in the abandoned church. Each artifact held a fragment of a story waiting to be told, yet no answers had yet surfaced.

Mia rubbed her temples, feeling the weight of fatigue settle heavily on her shoulders. The investigation was not just unearthing dark secrets; it was stirring memories of her own past—buried echoes she had tried to forget. She had hoped that returning to the force would provide a fresh start, a chance to prove herself again. Instead, as she sifted through Rebecca's life, she saw flickers of her own experience. The shadows of her past were relentless, whispering reminders of what it meant to be trapped and afraid.

Her phone buzzed, jolting her from her reverie. It was Peters. "Mia, I think you need to come down to the station. We've got something."

She sensed urgency in his voice and quickly grabbed her jacket, the cool fabric brushing against her skin as she stepped outside. The chill of the fall morning felt invigorating, a stark contrast to the oppressive atmosphere that had enveloped her at home.

Upon arriving at the precinct, she found Peters at his desk, a stack of papers in front of him. His face held a mixture of anxiety and determination. "I just got off the phone with Lila. She's scared, she thinks someone's been following her since we talked."

Mia's stomach twisted. "Did she say who?"

"No. Just that she saw a dark-haired man in a leather jacket lurking near her apartment last night." Peters leaned closer, lowering his voice. "She wanted to check in with us before she went to work."

"Good," Mia replied, her adrenaline spiking. "We need to stay in close contact with her. If she feels threatened, she should have a safe place to go."

Peters nodded, then pulled a file from under the pile of paperwork. "While I was talking to Lila, I did some digging into Rebecca's past. She had some trouble before moving here. A lot of her social media connections go back to a town called Marlowe."

Mia couldn't ignore the knot tightening in her chest. Marlowe; it was where she had grown up, a place filled with memories she had tried desperately to escape. "What did you find?"

"Rebecca was pretty active in her local community there—volunteering, making friends. But shortly before she moved to Ravenwood, a young man she dated went missing, and she stopped posting about her life there. It's like she vanished."

A wave of recognition washed over Mia. Memories began flooding back—Marlowe's dark corners, clandestine gatherings, a sense of foreboding that had loomed in the air long before she left. "Did anyone find out what happened to him?"

"No leads," Peters replied, rising to his feet. "But it's not the only dark thing associated with her past. I found records of a couple of incidents where she had sought help from local authorities. There were accusations of harassment linked to a group of men she had been seen with in Marlowe."

Mia felt the connection tighten, each piece lighting the way down a narrow corridor in her mind. "What group?"

"Some locals referred to them as 'The Brotherhood of Shadows.' Sound familiar?" Peters asked, searching for any hint of recognition in her face.

Her breath caught in her throat. "Yes... they were a part of the old cult's remaining influence. But they were thought to be gone years ago. Just whispers in the dark."

Mia felt the walls close in around her, and the weight of her own experiences began to resurface—a habitual cycle of silence and suffering that had become far too familiar. She had escaped Marlowe to free herself from the clutches of that darkness, yet here it was again, rearing its head.

"Maybe it's not just Rebecca's past we need to explore, but also the ties it has to the present," Mia said, resolving to dig deeper into both her own history and that of Rebecca, hoping it would unravel the tangled narrative before them. "We should go to Marlowe. I need to talk to people who knew her there."

"Are you sure?" Peters asked, concern etched across his features. "That could be risky. With Lila's situation, we need to stay focused."

"Exactly. Lila's plight is linked to Rebecca's past, and we can't afford to wait. If someone is targeting anyone related to Rebecca, we need to warn her and dig into these threads before they disappear."

THE DRIVE TO MARLOWE was filled with an uneasy silence, the landscape blurring past outside the car window. Mia's mind churned with apprehension and memories. Each mile felt like a journey into her own history, a path she had buried beneath layers of resolve.

Upon arriving, she felt the familiar weight of the air, thickened by familiar secrets. Marlowe had not changed much; its streets still retained that air of quiet despair. She parked near the town square, where quaint shops and cafes surrounded a statue that watched over the residents with an unsettling stillness.

"There's a small coffee shop—Beans & Brews—where Rebecca used to work, and a couple of her friends hung out," Peters stated as they exited the car.

Mia nodded, stealing herself against the tide of memories that threatened to overwhelm her. Together, they made their way through the late autumn bustle, shoppers navigating in and out of stores, laughter mingling with the crisp air. But beneath the surface, the currents felt charged.

As they entered the coffee shop, the warm aroma of roasted beans wrapped around her, stirring feelings of nostalgia. The barista, a young woman with a friendly smile, looked up as they approached.

"Can I help you?" she asked, her voice bright but her eyes cautious.

"We're looking for information on Rebecca Lane," Mia said, searching the woman's face for any flicker of recognition.

At the mention of Rebecca's name, the barista's expression shifted. "Oh... that poor girl. I heard what happened. What do you want to know?"

"Anything you can tell us about her. Friends? Relationships?" Peters pressed.

"Rebecca was loved here. She was sweet—always brightened our days. But after she started dating... well, it seemed to change her. She started hanging out with some different people, a few we didn't know well."

"You said she dated a guy before leaving town. Do you know anything about him?" Mia probed.

The barista hesitated, biting her lip. "Yes, John. He was... distant sometimes, a bit intense. When Rebecca broke up with him, he didn't take it well. Strange things happened in town after that—people saying they saw him lurking. Then he went missing."

The pieces began to fit together like a twisted puzzle. "Did the Brotherhood have any involvement with him?" Mia asked, the dread settling in her stomach.

"The Brotherhood? Oh, they've hung around for years. No one takes them seriously anymore, though. Just some old rumors. It's said they were obsessed with gathering power in town... and kept their fingers in everything." The barista's voice wavered. "People have whispered about them disappearing in the woods or calling on things no one should."

Mia's pulse quickened. Although she had evaded those shadows once, they were closing in now, each echo of the past resurfacing with haunting familiarity. This wasn't just about Rebecca anymore; it was about confronting the dark legacy that loomed over Marlowe.

"Where can we find John?" Peters asked, scanning the room for any signs of danger.

"I... I don't know. I heard he moved away after all the trouble. Last I heard, he was in a town nearby, maybe trying to keep a low profile."

As the barista offered to look up more information for them, Mia's mind raced with the implications. If he was lurking around, still entangled in past relationships with Rebecca, he could very well be part of the same dark tapestry woven by the Brotherhood.

As she looked at Peters, she understood that they were stepping closer to uncovering a truth that threatened to pull them under. Mia couldn't ignore the echoes of their past any longer; she needed to confront the shadows that had haunted her, and ensure that the cycle of silence and suffering ended with her.

With renewed determination, she prepared to dive deeper, ready to face her own history as they followed the threads that bound Rebecca, her past, and the chilling reality of the Brotherhood of Shadows together.

Chapter 10: The Art of Manipulation

The following days blurred together, each filled with aimless inquiries and the steadfast pursuit of answers that seemed perpetually out of reach. The deeper Mia Hart and her partner, Peters, dug into the labyrinthine history of the Cult of Shadows, the more they realized that the lines between victim and perpetrator were obscured by layers of deception.

As they sat in the precinct, poring over the journals unearthed at the abandoned church, a pattern began to emerge. The writings hinted at a philosophy rooted in control—control over oneself, over others, and ultimately, over life itself. The cult didn't just exist in the shadows; they thrived in manipulation, weaving a narrative that trapped individuals in a web of fear and loyalty.

"Mia, look at this." Peters pushed a page toward her, his voice low. "It talks about something called the 'Cleansing.' They believe that removing negative energies—sacrifice—can purify the community."

Mia's stomach churned as she read. "They think killing someone can wipe away their sins? This is sick."

"They've operated for decades," Peters replied, his focus intent. "The mention of rituals that date back generations suggests this isn't just a 'recent' thing. They're deeply rooted in this community."

Mia exhaled sharply, leaning back in her chair. "How do we even begin to counter a belief system like this? They're not just criminals; they're ideologues."

"By exposing their manipulation," Peters said, determination sparking in his eyes. "If we unravel their influence, we can cut the cord connecting them to the community. We need to investigate those who have been marked as 'lost' by their cryptic salvation."

Mia nodded, her mind racing. "Let's start with families of the missing. If they can help us understand how the cult operates, we might find a crack in their facade. Can you help set up some interviews?"

"Absolutely. I'll reach out to the families from the old missing persons' files," Peters replied, already typing notes into his laptop.

By the next week, they had assembled a list of potential interviewees—families of those who had disappeared over the years, rumored to have affiliations with the cult. Among those names was one that prickled Mia's senses: Sarah Quinn, a local woman whose daughter had vanished five years ago, just before Rebecca arrived in town.

As they prepared for the interview, Mia couldn't shake the feeling that they were stepping into the lion's den. The Cult of Shadows was not just a group of lost souls; they were skilled manipulators, using fear and hope interchangeably to bind their followers. It would take every ounce of her resolve to remain focused and not fall prey to their chilling allure.

The meeting took place in the small living room of Sarah Quinn's modest home, a space that felt like a time capsule, filled with photos of happier days and shadowed by grief. Sarah was a woman worn down by loss, her face etched with lines that told stories of sleepless nights and unanswered questions.

"Thank you for meeting with us, Sarah," Mia started, taking a seat across from the tight-lipped mother. "We're hoping to gather information about your daughter, Emily, and her connection to the Cult of Shadows."

Sarah's lips tightened, and for a moment, resentment flickered in her eyes. "If you're here to dredge up old wounds, you can leave. I've been through enough."

"Please, we understand your pain. We're here to seek justice—for Emily, and for others who've gone missing in Ravenwood," Peters added gently, sensing her hostility.

After a long silence, Sarah finally spoke, her voice barely a whisper. "Emily was enamored with the idea of finding purpose, community... and she thought the cult could provide that. I warned her, but she wouldn't listen."

"What do you mean by 'enamored'?" Mia pressed, her heart sinking at Sarah's pain. "Did she tell you things about them?"

"Only that they promised salvation, a way to transcend the ordinary," Sarah recounted, her eyes filled with unshed tears. "They manipulated her insecurities, convinced her she needed purification. I begged her to stay away."

"Did she ever talk about any specific rituals?" Peters asked, jotting down notes.

Sarah shook her head, frustration bubbling beneath her grief. "She became so distant... and once she disappeared, I learned that some believe a 'Cleansing' can help guide lost souls like hers. I knew the cult was involved, but the police didn't listen."

Mia exchanged glances with Peters, understanding the depth of Sarah's pain and frustration. "We believe that this cult uses emotional and psychological manipulation to recruit and control people. If you have any idea who she was close to within the cult, it could help."

At this, Sarah seemed to steel herself. "There was a man... Daniel something. He was one of the leaders. Charismatic but... dangerous. He could charm anyone into believing him."

"Do you have any information on him?" Mia asked, urgency creeping into her tone.

"Only that he used to hang around The Rusty Spoon. He had a way of making people feel seen, special. But I witnessed him turning from kind to cruel in a heartbeat. He had an uncanny ability to exploit weaknesses."

Mia felt a chill run through her. "Thank you for sharing this. Each piece helps us understand how they operate."

As they stood to leave, Mia caught a framed photo of Emily on the mantelpiece—a bright-eyed girl full of life, a haunting reminder of everything they were fighting for. "We'll do everything we can to find the truth," she promised Sarah, hoping to comfort the grieving mother.

Outside, the air was thick with unspoken horrors. As they walked to their car, Peters broke the silence. "This Daniel could be the key. If he's still involved, he might know more about Rebecca and those before her."

"Or he might be the catalyst that leads to more harm," Mia replied grimly. "We need to find out if he's still connected to the cult and, if so, how to approach him."

As they drove back to the precinct, Mia felt the encroaching shadows of the cult closing in around them. They were up against an enemy skilled in the art of manipulation—someone capable of dismantling their investigation before it even began. She needed to be strategic, but even more than that, she needed to remain one step ahead.

In the heart of the darkness, they had to expose the light—the truth that could break the cult's grip on the town. But she could already sense the lurking dangers, a foreboding promise that every thread unraveled would only tug tighter on the fabric of Ravenwood, pushing them both closer to a confrontation from which there might be no return.

Chapter 11: Beneath the Surface

The cold light of dawn broke over Ravenwood, illuminating a town still rattled by the previous night's revelations. Mia Hart stood by her kitchen window, her coffee untouched as she gazed out at the mist rising from the ground, cloaking the morning in a ghostly shroud. The atmosphere felt heavy, charged with anticipation, as if the town itself was holding its breath, waiting for something to be revealed.

She had spent the night poring over the journals she had taken from the abandoned church, their cryptic language haunting her thoughts. The more she read, the clearer it became that the Cult of Shadows had deeply embedded roots in Ravenwood, elders manipulating events from the shadows, orchestrating a play she was only beginning to understand.

Her phone buzzed violently on the table, jolting her from her reverie. It was Peters. "Mia, get over here. We have a lead."

Mia raced to her car, her heart racing not just with urgency but with the adrenaline of the chase. The precinct was buzzing with activity when she arrived, officers darting from desk to desk, their faces taut with determination. Peters waved her over, his expression a mixture of excitement and anxiety.

"What did you find?" she asked, catching her breath.

"I spoke with some locals who frequent The Rusty Spoon. One of them recognized the guy who was fixated on Rebecca. He's been in and out of town recently, and one of them overheard him mentioning some sort of gathering out by the old quarry. They said he was involved with the cult but never confirmed it until now."

"Do we have a name?" Mia felt her pulse quicken.

"Yeah. It's Nick Voss. I looked up some records, and it turns out he has a criminal history—assault, harassment, and disturbing the peace." Peters leaned closer, his voice low. "He was in and out of juvenile detention a few years back, but nobody in town seems to know much about what he's up to now."

"Perfect," Mia said, already formulating a plan. "We need to track him down. If he's connected to Rebecca, he might know what happened to her."

They quickly drafted a plan, gathering intelligence on Voss's whereabouts while simultaneously cross-referencing his known associates with the cult. The sun had climbed higher in the sky, illuminating the cobwebs of secrecy that tangled the townsfolk tighter than ever before.

LATER THAT AFTERNOON, they arrived at the old quarry—a jagged expanse of land that jutted out of the earth like the remains of a forgotten monument. It was a site where the townspeople once played, but over the years it had transformed into a clandestine meeting spot rumored to be favored by cult members.

Mia and Peters parked their car on a gravelly incline, the crunch of stones beneath their feet echoing in the stillness. The air felt thick with foreboding, the remains of the day's warmth giving way to a creeping chill.

"Do you think anyone will be here?" Peters asked, scanning the terrain, the jagged rocks casting long shadows.

"Beats me," Mia replied, pulling out her flashlight. "But we can't take any chances. Let's stay low and see what we can find."

As they approached the edge of the quarry, the world around them fell silent, as if the landscape itself was attuned to their presence. Suddenly, Mia spotted movement. She nudged Peters, and they crept closer, crouching behind a cluster of boulders.

In the clearing below, a group of figures gathered around a makeshift bonfire. Clad in dark clothing, they stood in a circle, faces obscured by shadows and hoods. The flickering flames danced against the night, casting long, distorted shapes that added to the air of menace.

Mia pulled out her phone, recording silently as she watched. The crackle of the fire mingled with the low hum of a chant—familiar words she had read in the journals, twisted and interwoven into an incantation.

Her heart raced as she recognized the leader's voice rising above the others, a deep, resonant timbre that commanded attention. "We gather in the name of the shadows," he intoned, "to reclaim the lost and to call forth those who have strayed from our sides. Blood unites us, and blood will bind our fates..."

Suddenly, she felt a sharp nudge against her shoulder. Peters leaned closer. "We need to call for backup," he whispered urgently.

"Not yet," Mia replied, her eyes glued to the scene before her. "Let's see what they're planning first."

As she recorded silently, a familiar figure stepped into view, his grim features enveloped in the fire's glow. It was Nick Voss. Her stomach dropped as she recognized him from the diner's surveillance footage—his dark hair, his piercing gaze now fixed on the flickering flames.

"The girl," Nick said loudly, his voice cutting through the chant. "She has awakened something that we cannot control. We must act, or we will be consumed!"

A ripple of murmurs cascaded through the group, tension mounting in the air thick with anxiety. "She must pay the price for her transgressions," another voice chimed in—a high-pitched whisper that sent a chill down Mia's spine.

Mia's mind raced. "They're talking about Rebecca," she breathed, horror gripping her heart. "They think she exposed them somehow. We need to—"

Before she could finish, a rustle behind them broke the spell of silence. Peters tensed, hand instinctively moving toward his holstered weapon. But as he turned, their cover was blown. A figure emerged from the shadows, eyes wide and wild.

"It's too late!" the figure shouted, recognition dawning. It was one of the locals from the diner—Jared, a young man with disheveled hair and frantic eyes. "You can't stop them! They'll kill you!"

"Jared, what are you doing here?" Peters demanded, confusion mingled with urgency.

"They're going to sacrifice her!" Jared's words tumbled out in a panic. "Rebecca's in danger. I tried to warn her—she thought it was just a party. They won't let anyone stop them!"

Mia felt her heart drop as the pieces of the puzzle fell into place—Rebecca hadn't just vanished; she had been lured into this madness. "We need to get help," she said, adrenaline surging through her veins. "Right now."

"I can't—" Jared choked, eyes darting to the cult gathering below. "They'll know. They'll see us. You have to go. You have to save her!"

"I won't leave you," Peters replied, tense and focused.

Without warning, the chanting intensified, the group moving in a synchronized dance around the fire, their bodies swaying dangerously close to the flames. In that moment, something shifted within Mia—a resolve igniting like a flame in her chest.

"We find a way to distract them," she hissed, adrenaline coursing through her. "We create a diversion. You stay with Jared. Get help!"

As the shadows thickened around them, Mia felt the weight of a decision pressing down on her. The darkness was tangible, a heavy presence threatening to consume everything. But beneath the surface lay a truth waiting to be unearthed—one that, despite the odds, she would fight to bring into the light.

"Trust me," she said, meeting Peters' gaze with fierce determination. "I'll bring her back."

As she dashed into the thickening night, the flickering flames cast a path through the darkness, illuminating her resolve as she prepared to confront the malevolent force that had coiled around Ravenwood, threatening to pull them all into the abyss.

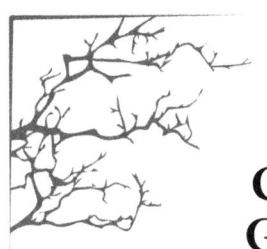

Chapter 12: The Gathering Storm

The sky over Ravenwood was an ominous slate gray, heavy clouds swirling like an angry ocean. Mia stood at her window, watching the forecasted storm brew in the distance. She could feel a tight knot of unease building within her as thunder rumbled softly, a prelude to the tempest that mirrored the turmoil swirling in her investigation.

It had been nearly two weeks since Rebecca's murder, and the layers of the case had only grown thicker and darker. Reports of missing persons began to trickle in, painted in the same disquieting strokes as Rebecca's story. Each new victim was a reminder that something sinister lingered just beneath the surface of the town.

"Do you think it's all connected?" Peters asked, standing beside her, staring out at the churning clouds. "The cult, the murders... the disappearances?"

Mia sighed, her gaze fixed on the horizon. "There's a pattern emerging, but we still need more concrete evidence before we can connect the dots. I have a feeling the storm isn't just meteorological. It's about to break, and we need to be ready."

"Right," Peters nodded, tapping a pen against his notepad. "What's the plan?"

"First, we need to gather any reports or leads on the missing people. We'll start interviewing their families, see if there's been any mention of strange behavior or cult activity." She turned to face him, determination etched in her expression. "We also need to check in with Lila again. She might remember something new."

Before they could proceed, the phone rang, slicing through the tension. Mia answered, her heart racing as she recognized Deputy Stone's voice on the other end.

"Mia, we've got a problem," he said, urgency lacing his tone. "There's been another disappearance. A girl named Sarah Lind, eighteen years old. Last seen leaving a party near the park."

Mia's stomach twisted. "When was she last seen?"

"Last night. Witnesses say she left the party around midnight and was headed toward Miller's Park. No one's heard from her since."

"She fits the same profile as Rebecca," Peters interjected, his eyes widening. "We need to act fast."

"Where are the eyewitnesses?" Mia asked, scribbling down notes as she spoke.

"They're at the station now, but you should hurry. The family is distraught, and I think we might catch something fresh from them."

"I'm on my way," Mia said, her heart pounding with urgency.

They arrived at the precinct, where a small crowd of anxious faces filled the waiting area. The tension was palpable—frantic whispers and muffled sobs echoed off the walls, amplifying the already heavy atmosphere.

Deputy Stone met them at the door, relief washing over him as he led them to a small conference room. "The family is in here. They've been waiting for someone to talk to them."

Mia took a breath, steeling herself before stepping inside. The Lind family sat around a table, their anguish etched into their faces. The mother, a woman with tear-stained cheeks and trembling hands, looked up, her eyes filled with desperation.

"Please, you have to find her," Mrs. Lind pleaded, her voice breaking. "Sarah wouldn't just disappear. Something happened to her."

"We're doing everything we can," Mia reassured her, keeping her tone steady and compassionate. "Can you tell us about the last time you saw her?"

The father, a stoic figure with a furrowed brow, spoke next. "She came home from school early, said something about hanging out with friends. We knew she was going to a party, but she promised she'd be home by midnight. When she didn't come back..." He hesitated, biting back the emotion that threatened to overwhelm him.

"Do you know where the party was?" Peters asked, leaning forward. "Anyone unusual there? Any boys she might have been talking to?"

Mrs. Lind shook her head, her eyes wide with fear. "She mentioned a new friend... some boy she met online. Said he was going to be at the party. That's all I know."

Mia exchanged a glance with Peters, a sense of foreboding creeping in. "Do you have his name or any contact information?"

The family's tragic silence hung heavy in the air, a stark testament to Sarah's absence. "No... she didn't give us any details. We assumed it was normal," the father said, frustration mixing with despair. "Now we wish we had asked more questions."

"We'll speak to her friends," Mia promised, her voice firm. "If they knew anything, they must know who this boy is. We'll leave no stone unturned."

With empathy weighing heavily on her heart, she and Peters stepped out of the room. "We need to get back to Lila," she said. "If Sarah connected with someone online, maybe Rebecca did too. We can't discount the possibility of a link between these girls."

As they drove to the diner, the storm began to unleash its fury, pouring sheets of rain that blurred the world around them. Mia felt the tension in the air shift, an ominous portent of danger that merged with the urgency of their task.

Inside The Rusty Spoon, the atmosphere was filled with hushed conversations, the regulars a mix of concern and curiosity. Lila sat in a booth, her usual brightness dulled by shadows of grief. When she spotted Mia and Peters, her expression shifted to one of hope.

"Mia! What's going on? Is it about Sarah?" she asked, her voice a fragile tremor.

"Unfortunately, yes," Mia replied, taking a seat across from her. "We're trying to figure out if anything connects Sarah to Rebecca's case. Have you learned anything new since we last talked?"

Lila shook her head, her hands fidgeting nervously with the edge of the table. "I've been searching online. Trying to find anything... but I don't know what I'm looking for. It's like they vanished."

Mia leaned closer, the urgency brimming in her chest. "Lila, was there anything at the party Sarah mentioned? Anyone she talked about a lot, maybe a new friendship?"

Lila's brow furrowed. "Just that boy she met online... but I didn't think Sarah was serious about him. It was just a fling. She didn't say his name, but she did say he was different. I remember her mentioning he was part of some group..."

"Group? What kind of group?" Peters pressed.

Lila hesitated, her gaze dropping to her hands. "Something about a community... or a club. She said they had a 'special interest' in the paranormal. But it was all in jest. You know how girls are—just like to make fun of things like that."

"Lila, this isn't just innocent fun anymore," Mia said, her voice firm with resolve. "We need to treat this seriously. Can you think of anything else?"

"Maybe... she did mention a website where they shared stories. Wait." Lila's eyes widened as if recalling a spark of memory. "There was something else—a meetup. Some gathering in the woods around the full moon."

Mia's heart raced as clarity started to form in her mind. "We need to find out more about this gathering. It might lead us to Sarah and the others."

As the rain fell in torrents outside, a collective sense of dread filled the diner. A storm was indeed gathering, but this one was born not of nature but of something far darker.

The details were falling into place, but Mia could feel the pressure in her chest as if the very air were thick with impending violence. Time was slipping away, and if they didn't act quickly, the tempest of secrets could claim more victims before the night was through.

"Let's move," she said, adrenaline surging through her. "We need to find this meetup before it's too late."

With that, they braced themselves against the storm—both outside and within the shadows lurking in their town—determined to bring the truth to light before darkness claimed yet another innocent life.

Chapter 13: Breaking Point

The hum of the fluorescent lights above felt like a relentless drone, gnawing at Mia Hart's sanity. She sat in the dimly lit interrogation room of the precinct, surrounded by the remnants of paperwork spread across the table: police reports, witness statements, and the journals she had unearthed from the Cult of Shadows' church. Each page held more shadows than light, tales of despair and manipulation that seeped into her consciousness, warping her sense of reality.

Days had slipped by in a blur, each hour layered with dread and urgency. With Rebecca's murder still unsolved, the weight of expectation pressed down on Mia like a suffocating fog. The town was on edge, and rumors rattled through Ravenwood like leaves in a winter breeze. As she poured over the evidence again, every word felt like a whisper, taunting her with the darkness she had yet to unravel.

Peters pushed the door open, his face pale and drawn. "Mia, you need to see this."

She looked up, her heart accelerating at the gravity in his voice. "What is it?"

Peters dropped a manila folder on the table with a thud. "Another body was found... same markings as Rebecca."

"Oh God, not again." Fear clawed at her throat. "Where?"

"Just a few miles from the park, near the old mill. The victim's a young woman, early twenties, just like Rebecca. The markings—they match what we found in the journals. This isn't coincidence."

Anger mixed with despair surged through Mia as she fought the overwhelming urge to scream. "How can this be happening again? We need to let people know about the cult! They can't just keep picking off young women in this town! We can't let more blood be shed!"

Peters shook his head vehemently. "We can't panic the public without solid proof. We'd create chaos and could even scare the cult into hiding—into doing something worse."

She had fought this battle with him before, but seeing the weight of their failures hanging in the air felt unbearable. "What's left to wait for, Peters? Another victim?"

"What do you want me to do? We need to gather enough evidence to take down whoever is responsible."

"Evidence?" Mia snapped. "We've had evidence, but it's been hidden beneath layers of fear and secrecy! This cult has festered in the shadows for years while we sit here playing by the book!"

"We need to follow protocol. It's our only chance of—"

"Of what? Of sitting on our hands until it's too late?" She stood, fists clenched, heart pounding. "I'm done waiting. I'm done being careful. Someone has to take action before it's too late."

"Mia!" His voice broke, rising in urgency as she turned to storm out. "We can't afford to lose you too! You're teetering on a breaking point! This is already messing with your head—you need to take a step back!"

But Mia couldn't hear him over the deafening roar of desperation. Her mind was clouded with the realities of what lay ahead, and she couldn't let this chance slip by. The cult wasn't just a group of misguided individuals; it threatened the very fabric of her town, and within its twisted rituals lay the key to stopping the violence.

She stormed out of the precinct, the cold night air hitting her like a slap. The streets, normally familiar and welcoming, felt alien and foreboding. She had to push through this feeling of isolation and despair. There was something deep within her—perhaps a primal instinct—that urged her to dig deeper, to confront this darkness head-on.

Her first stop was The Rusty Spoon. Lila's face hadn't left her thoughts. The girl had been a beacon in the darkness, showing the way to potential allies against the cult. As she entered the diner, the warm glow from inside was both comforting and suffocating.

As she approached the counter, she spotted Lila sitting alone, her eyes puffy from crying but resolute. Mia felt a surge of determination. "Lila, I need your help."

Lila blinked, surprise coloring her features. "Mia? I thought you would be busy with the investigation."

"Busy enough that I could use another set of eyes," Mia replied, her voice low and urgent. "There's been another murder. I need to know everything you can about Rebecca's life, her friends... anyone who might have been involved with that guy, or the cult."

"I don't know much..." Lila said haltingly. "But I can try. I just... I might be risking more than I'm ready for."

"I know it's dangerous, but I need you to trust me. The stakes are too high now. We can't let this happen again."

They shared a tense moment, the weight of their situation looming over them. "Okay. I'll help," Lila finally said. "But we need a plan. I'm scared."

"Good," Mia breathed. "That fear can be a powerful motivator. We'll find out what we need to know, and we'll do it together."

As evening settled in, they began to piece together Rebecca's life bit by bit, sharing stories, names, and connections. They called friends and acquaintances, delving into phone logs and social media accounts, creating a list of individuals who had crossed paths with Rebecca shortly before her death.

Mia's phone buzzed, pulling her from their investigative discussions. It was a text from Peters: *We need to meet. Urgent.*

"Lila, I have to go meet Peters. Keep digging, okay? I'll be back as soon as I can."

Once outside, the creeping anxiety returned. What had Peters discovered? She felt as though she was walking a tightrope, the reality of the case stretching her beyond her limits. Each new layer of darkness that revealed itself threatened to fracture her fragile control.

When she reached the precinct, Peters was pacing, agitated. "Mia, we have a problem. The body—"

"What about it?" she pressed impatiently, fear hanging like a fog in the air.

"Wasn't just a random girl. She's connected to Lila. Her name was Carly Steele. They were best friends back in their last town."

The floor dropped from beneath her. "How do we know this isn't just coincidence?"

"We don't." Peters ran a hand through his hair, frustration evident. "But we need to get Lila out of town. Now. If they're targeting her, she could be next."

"No," Mia shot back. "Lila's invested now. We can't just run."

"Are you serious?" His voice cracked with desperation. "This isn't a game! This is someone's life—we don't even know what these people are capable of!"

"This detective work is my life!" she shouted, feeling the breaking point creep into her voice. "I can't walk away while we chase shadows. I won't let this cult win."

Tension thickened between them, a palpable moment where neither was willing to back down. But Mia could feel it—the pressure building, the cracks widening beneath their facade of control.

"Mia," Peters said quietly, taking a step closer, his tone shifting from anger to concern. "I know you want justice for Rebecca. We all do. But you're not alone in this. We need each other now more than ever."

For a moment, vulnerability flashed across Mia's face—a flicker of the girl still within her, the one who had lost her way. But just as quickly, she set her jaw, steeling herself against that vulnerability. "Then we fight together. In this town, we'll uncover the truth. No matter what it takes."

As she gripped Peter's arm, determination ignited within her once more. The line between darkness and light was thin, and they were standing on the brink. Together, they would confront this nightmare head-on before it consumed not just Lila, but the entire town.

Nothing would stand in their way. It was time to turn the tide against the shadows whispering through Ravenwood, and Mia felt the strength of her resolve harden like steel. The coming confrontation with the Cult of Shadows would either break her or forge her anew. But she was ready, ready to face the darkness head-on, no matter the cost.

Chapter 14: Truth in Blood

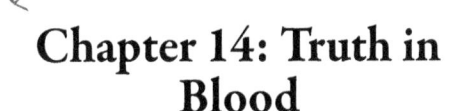

The next few days passed in a blur of activity for Detective Mia Hart and Officer Peters. With each piece of evidence they uncovered, the interconnected threads of the Cult of Shadows tightened around them like a noose. The deeper they delved, the more ominous the forecast became. Local residents were on edge, whispers transforming into urgent murmurs as the cold grip of fear descended upon Ravenwood.

Mia sat at her desk, sifting through the pile of journals and documents recovered from the abandoned church. Her head pounded as she attempted to make sense of the chaotic disarray of rituals, names, and chilling prophecies. The freshly printed photographs of Rebecca Lane were pinned to the corkboard above her desk, staring back at her with vacant eyes—their lifelessness a constant reminder of what was at stake.

"Detective Hart." Peters' voice broke through the silence, pulling her from her thoughts.

Mia looked up to see him standing at her door, holding a folder. "What do you have?"

He stepped inside, his expression serious. "We managed to enhance some surveillance footage from the park the night Rebecca was killed. Take a look."

Mia leaned forward as Peters set the folder on the desk, revealing a series of stills depicting a dark figure lurking near the park entrance. The figure matched Lila's description of the man who had watched Rebecca at the diner. The shadows obscured much of his features, but there was something unnervingly familiar about his build.

"Can we identify him?" she asked, analyzing the images closely.

"We're running facial recognition through the database now, but we've got something else. One of the young officers canvassing the area found a witness who claims they heard chanting coming from the park just before the incident."

"Chanting?" Mia frowned, the weight of dread settling into her bones. "Could it have been a ritual?"

"Possibly. The witness wasn't able to see anything, but they described a procession of figures moving toward the old stone circle at the heart of the park. We need to get there. They might still be using it for their ceremonies."

Mia's heart raced at the thought. She stood up, adrenaline coursing through her veins. "Let's go. If there's any chance they're planning something, we need to confront them."

THE SUN DIPPED LOW as they made their way to the park. Mia and Peters parked a distance away to avoid drawing attention. The low light cast eerie shadows among the trees, the path ahead cloaked in mystery. The air felt electric, charged with a tension that made the hair on the back of Mia's neck stand on end.

"We should split up," she suggested, scanning the area. "If they're out here, we'll have a better chance of discovering what's really happening if we cover more ground."

Peters agreed, though his expression betrayed his concern. "Just be careful. We have no idea how many of them there could be."

With a nod, Mia ventured deeper into the underbrush, her flashlight cutting through the gloom. The faint sound of rustling leaves

… and distant murmurs reached her ears, growing louder as she approached the stone circle—a remnant from a time when the town had been a sanctuary for rituals far removed from darkness.

As she rounded a thick tree, the ancient stones came into view, their jagged silhouettes ominous against the twilight sky. Mia crouched behind a bush, peering through the branches. What she saw made her breath hitch in her throat.

A gathering of hooded figures encircled the stones, flickering candles forming a ring around them. Their voices melded into a haunting chant, words she couldn't quite make out but that resonated with a sense of urgency. The atmosphere crackled like static electricity, filled with an energy that sent chills down her spine.

"Mia..." came Peters' whisper from behind her, startling her as he crouched down beside her. "This is it."

They watched as one figure stepped forward, raising their arms to the night sky, a commanding presence in the throng. The shadows shifted, and for a brief moment, the hood slipped back, revealing the face of the cult leader—the enigmatic figure known as The Seer.

"Blood will cleanse the past," The Seer proclaimed, their voice cutting through the night like a knife. "In sacrifice, we will find rebirth. Our strength lies in the shadows, our power in the void. Tonight, we reveal our new beginnings!"

Mia felt the blood drain from her face. They were planning something. The urgency of the cult's purpose crystallized into a single, horrifying truth: they were not merely a group lost in ritual; they were a danger to the very fabric of the town.

"Should we move in?" Peters asked, his adrenaline surging as he gripped his flashlight.

"Not yet," Mia whispered back. "We need to listen. They could have more planned than just words."

The chanting continued, swelling in intensity. Suddenly, a new figure emerged from the shadows, her wrists bound with rope. The gasps from the gathering echoed in Mia's ears, realizing the young woman was Lila. Her eyes were wide with fear, and she struggled against her restraints as she was brought to the center of the circle.

"Let her go!" Peters hissed, his restraint barely holding.

"No," Mia urged, her senses hyper-aware. "If we act now, we could put Lila in even greater danger."

The Seer turned toward Lila, their demeanor now dripping with malevolence. "You sought the truth, my dear. But truth has a price. You will be the vessel through which we will resurrect our power. The shadows will guide us."

Mia's heart raced. She couldn't let this happen. The culmination of fear, anger, and desperation surged within her.

"Enough!" she shouted, breaking from her cover as Peters followed her lead.

The cultists turned, confusion morphing into rage as they processed the intrusion. The shadows shifted, revealing their twisted faces.

"What is this?" The Seer snapped, eyes narrowing at Mia.

"Your ritual ends here," Mia declared, adrenaline coursing through her veins. "Release her, now!"

"Fools!" The Seer gestured to the others, and the air crackled with tension as they prepared to strike.

Without thinking, Peters rushed forward, pushing past Mia to shield her and Lila. "We're the law! Drop the knives!" he yelled, brandishing his flashlight like a weapon.

The cultists hesitated, the fear of discovery settling into their ranks. In that split second of uncertainty, Mia grabbed Lila's arm, pulling her toward safety. "Come on!"

They stumbled back, retreating from the circle just as Peters engaged with the cult members. It was chaos—a clash of shouting, flashing lights, and the palpable energy of desperation.

Mia and Lila darted behind a tree just as a cult member lunged at them. Peters' voice rang out, firm and commanding. "Get down! Back away!"

Mia turned to Lila, heart pounding. "Are you hurt?"

"No, just scared," Lila replied, tears streaming down her face.

"Stay low. We'll get you out of this."

Mia peered around the tree, heart racing as the clash unfolded. The shadows of the cult danced erratically, flickering with the chaos. She could see a few of the members breaking ranks, scattered in confusion.

"Peters, we need backup!" she shouted, adrenaline surging through her.

Just as she said that, a flurry of sirens pierced the night, illuminating the park as squad cars raced toward them, headlights shining into the chaos.

The Seer's voice rose above the clamor as they raised their arms, but it was too late. The gathering was disbanding under the weight of law enforcement, the moment of reverie shattered by the rush of reality. The cultists scattered, fleeing into the dark underbrush of the park.

"Lila, come on!" Mia pulled her hand, and they sprinted toward Peters, who was now covering them as they escaped into the safety of the trees.

"Get Lila out of here!" Peters shouted, taking defensive postures as the last cultists slipped away into the shadows.

Mia nodded, her focus sharp. "We have to report this! They could regroup!"

As the police descended on the park, the remnants of the night began to unravel, but the truth was already spilling out. They hadn't just stumbled upon a gathering; they had uncovered the dark underbelly of Ravenwood—the blood that had been spilled for the sake of power, the lives tethered to a cult thriving in the shadows.

As they emerged from the darkness, dodging the confusion of flashing lights and frantic voices, Mia realized that the truth was more than just a story waiting to be told; it was soaked in blood—Rebecca's blood, Lila's blood—and they would uncover every last mystery that linked this town to the Cult of Shadows.

Chapter 15: The Final Rites

The night was heavy with anticipation, the air thick with the scent of damp earth and the faintest hint of incense lingering like a ghost. Mia Hart stood at the edge of Miller's Park, where the moon hung low, casting silver beams that danced on the surface of the grass. Shadows shifted between the trees, and somewhere in the depths of the night, she could hear the murmur of voices rising like a haunting hymn.

Tonight was the night.

After weeks of unraveling the threads that connected Rebecca Lane to the sinister Cult of Shadows, Mia knew the cult planned to perform their final rites—a culmination of their dark rituals that would mark a significant event. Whether it was a new member's initiation or a sacrificial offering, she couldn't be certain, but she was determined to put a stop to it.

"Are you sure about this?" Peters asked, adjusting his gear as they stood in the underbrush at the park's edge. The flickering glow of candles could be seen through the trees, illuminating figures clad in dark robes.

"We need to document everything and find out who's leading this," Mia whispered, her heart pounding in her chest. "This could be our chance to put an end to them."

The two of them crouched lower behind the undergrowth, watching as members of the cult gathered. The air was electric, charged with a sense of purpose as the figures formed a circle around a central firepit, laden with offerings that looked grotesque in the flickering light—dried herbs, animal bones, and something else that sent a shiver down Mia's spine.

"Look," Peters murmured, pointing toward the center. "It's the Seer."

Through the shadows, a tall figure stepped forward, their face obscured by a dark hood. The Seer's voice rose above the murmurs, commanding and resonant. "Tonight, we honor the blood that binds us, the shadows that guide us. The time has come to embrace our true purpose."

Mia felt a chill wash over her. This had to be the same leader they had glimpsed in the faded photographs from the church. They had found their puppet master, the person pulling the strings behind the dark scenes of Ravenwood.

"Let's get a closer look," Mia insisted, her determination igniting a fire within her. She motioned for Peters to follow as they moved silently through the undergrowth, inching closer to the flickering light and the gathering cult.

As they crept forward, Mia's heart raced. Each step echoed the tension in her mind. They were treading dangerously close to the edge, exposing themselves to whatever darkness lay ahead.

Suddenly, a sharp sound split the air—a small branch snapping beneath her foot. Time froze, and every head turned toward the sound, the air thick with suspicion.

"Who goes there?" The Seer's voice echoed, laced with authority.

Mia exchanged a frantic glance with Peters, adrenaline coursing through her veins. She motioned for him to stay quiet as she pressed backward, hoping to retreat before they were exposed. But then, she felt a tug at her sleeve—Peters was still frozen in place, anguish on his face as he caught the attention of cult members.

"Get ready," Mia hissed, heart racing as she pulled her phone from her pocket, already dialing for backup.

Before she could finish the call, the Seer raised a hand. "Bring the intruders to me. We shall see if their blood sings the same song as ours."

Chaos erupted as cult members moved toward them, their dark forms swarming through the trees. Peters grabbed Mia's arm, urging her to run. "We can't let them catch us!"

They sprinted through the woods, their hearts pounding in tandem with their footsteps. The distant fire grew dimmer, the voices now a cacophony of anger and confusion behind them. They needed to reach safety, to regroup.

"Over there!" Mia shouted, pointing toward a narrow escape route that led to an old shed used in the park, a remnant of simpler times. They ducked inside just as the shadows loomed closer, the sounds of shuffling feet echoing outside.

Inside the shed, silence enveloped them. They took a moment to catch their breath, the adrenaline beginning to ebb as the reality of their vulnerability settled in.

"Mia, what's the plan?" Peters whispered, eyeing the door as if it might burst open at any moment.

"We can't fight them head-on. We need to gather evidence, expose them." Mia leaned closer, lowering her voice. "There's likely a document or transfer of power—they often leave trails."

Just then, the shed's door creaked, and the dark shapes of cult members slipped inside. "Search everywhere!" commanded a voice. "They can't have gone far!"

Mia and Peters were pressed against a wall, holding their breath as the searchers turned the shed upside down. Tension crackled in the air like static electricity, and the warmth of the moment was quickly replaced by cold dread.

Suddenly, one of the cultists stepped too close to Mia's hiding spot, their shadow looming. Peters shifted, trying to reposition himself silently, but it was too late. The cultist's eyes widened, and in an instant, the alarm was raised.

"They're here!" the cultist shouted, lunging toward them.

"Run!" Mia barked, pushing Peters towards the door as they darted out into the night. They raced back into the forest, the shadows now alive with pursuit, their panting breaths echoing against the trees.

As they navigated the underbrush, they heard voices growing louder, the cult members fracturing into groups to search for them. The darkness was closing in; their only hope lay in reaching the nearby road where they could call for help.

But then, the path ahead opened up into a clearing, and in that moment, Mia saw it—the focal point of the cult's ritual, a large stone altar. The remnants of previous ceremonies still marked the surface, smeared with the remnants of offerings long gone.

"This is it," Mia said, her voice steadying with purpose. "If we can gather evidence here, we can expose them once and for all."

As they rushed forward, the Seer's voice rang out again, cutting through the chaos of the night. "Stop! You cannot escape judgment!"

The urgency of their actions rose as they reached the altar, the shadows swirling around them, blending into the dark. They needed to find something—anything that could link the cult to Rebecca's death, something to drag their secrets into the light.

"Look," Peters shouted, pulling free a tattered piece of fabric caught on a jagged stone. As he lifted it, Mia recognized its color—a distinct shade of blue she had seen in Rebecca's belongings.

"That belongs to her!" she exclaimed, her mind racing. "If we can get pictures of this..."

But before they could think further, members of the cult surged into the clearing from all sides. "Seize them!" the Seer commanded, their presence looming like a dark cloud.

Mia grabbed Peters' arm. "We have to go, now!"

They turned to run, but the crowd of shadows closed in fast. Just as they reached the edge of the clearing, the Seer's voice rang out again, commanding and omnipotent. "You may flee, but the shadows always linger; they will spill your blood if you do not submit to us!"

Panic surged through Mia as she pushed Peters ahead of her. "Keep moving, don't look back!"

They raced through the trees, branches snagging at their clothes as they navigated the labyrinth of trunks and leaves. Mia's mind spun with terror and determination—she knew the danger they faced, but she also knew that if they survived, they would expose the cult and the darkness that had claimed Rebecca.

Bursts of light sparked in the distance, and she realized they were approaching the road again, desperation fueling their escape. Just a little further...

Finally, they burst out into the open, breathless and almost in tears at the sight of the empty road, headlights approaching from the horizon.

They turned to run toward it, waving their arms in desperation. "Help! Please!" Mia shouted, the adrenaline still coursing through her veins.

As the headlights drew closer, Mia took one last look back into the shadows where the cult members had been. The whispers of the night surged like a tempest around her, the echo of their chants intertwining with the wild rhythm of her heart. She realized the final rites were not just for Rebecca, but for Ravenwood itself—a town on the brink of darkness.

In that moment of escape, a single thought crystallized in her mind: they had awakened something ancient and sinister, but tonight, they had also taken their first step toward bringing the truth into the light. And she would not rest until the shadows were cast out for good.

Chapter 16: Into Darkness

The moon hung low in the night sky, a spectral orb casting an eerie glow over Ravenwood. Mia Hart stood at the edge of Miller's Park, the very place where Rebecca Lane had lost her life. The air was thick with tension, and each rustle of leaves felt like a warning. Tonight was no ordinary night; it was the night of the cult's ritual, a grim convergence that promised to unveil secrets buried in blood.

Mia had spent the last few days unraveling the threads of the Cult of Shadows, speaking to locals, gathering snippets of information that painted a dark portrait of a group steeped in ancient practices and manipulation. Now, she felt the weight of those discoveries pressing down on her like a vice. If she was going to infiltrate the cult, she would need to tread carefully.

"Are you sure about this?" Peters asked, his voice low and laced with concern as they crouched behind the trees bordering the park. He adjusted his earpiece, his face barely illuminated by the red glow of his tactical flashlight. "This isn't a game, Mia."

"I'm not taking this lightly. We need to know what they're planning," she replied, steeling her resolve. She could feel the adrenaline coursing through her body, sharpening her senses. Time was of the essence, and the thought of Rebecca's life stolen at the hands of this malevolent group fueled her determination.

The makeshift altar had been set up at the heart of the park, surrounded by flickering candlelight. Dark figures moved with purposeful intent, their voices murmuring incantations that echoed through the night. Mia could see the familiar faces of some Ravenwood residents intermingled among the robed figures, a twisted display of trust and betrayal that sent chills down her spine.

"We should call for backup," Peters urged, eyes darting around for potential threats. "If this goes sideways—"

"And risk alerting them?" Mia shot back, her voice barely above a whisper but fierce. "We can't take that chance. We need to hear what they're saying first."

Taking a deep breath, she peered through the foliage, watching as the cult members arranged themselves around the altar. The cult leader, cloaked in shadows, stood at the center, his presence dominating. He raised his arms like a conductor preparing for an orchestra, and silence fell over the assembly.

"Brothers and sisters," he intoned, his voice deep and resonant, "tonight we summon the strength of the shadows that bind us. We celebrate the blood that has been spilled in our name." He gestured dramatically toward a bowl that rested on the altar, dark liquid glistening in the candlelight.

Mia's stomach twisted as she recognized the blood—a ritual sacrifice. "They're planning to sacrifice someone," she whispered to Peters, urgency creeping into her voice. "We can't let that happen."

"We need to move, Mia. If you make a scene—"

But she was already stepping forward, her resolve unwavering. This was bigger than her own fears. The cult had taken a life, and the depths of darkness they operated within had to be exposed. "I'll create a diversion. You need to get evidence and call for backup."

Peters hesitated. "Mia, wait—"

But she was already disappearing into the shadows, heart pounding with each step. She crept around the edge of the clearing, focusing on the chants that filled the air, drawing strength from the shadows that enveloped her. Their words morphed into a haunting melody, tugging at her senses, but she shook off the effect. She needed clarity, not the intoxicating pull of their dark energy.

Finding a nearby tree, she climbed up quickly, edging along a low-hanging branch that hung directly above the altar. From this vantage point, she could see everything unfold beneath her. The members raised their arms in supplication, chanting in a language she didn't recognize, but the intent was clear.

Suddenly, the crowd parted as a young woman was brought forward—unconscious and restrained, the victim of the night's brutal intention. Mia's heart sank. "No! Not again..."

"Tonight, we honor the sacrifices made for our awakening," the leader called, raising the bowl of dark liquid toward the sky. "With this offering, we shall transcend and free our souls from the bindings of the mortal realm!"

Mia felt her heart race as she drew out her phone, fingers shaking as she activated the camera. "I've got to record this," she muttered, positioning her lens to capture the harrowing scene below.

But before she could hit 'record,' a chilling hand landed on her shoulder, gripping tightly. She gasped and whirled around, facing a hooded figure emerging from the shadows behind her. The figure was cloaked, eyes barely visible beneath the fabric, but Mia could feel the sinister energy radiating from them.

"You shouldn't be here," the figure hissed, their voice a warning and a threat.

Mia fought her instincts to flee, her mind racing for a plan. "I'm here to stop this! You don't have to do this."

A laugh echoed softly, unnervingly calm. "You think you can interrupt a ritual meant to elevate us? You've walked into the heart of darkness, and you will be consumed."

Mia's pulse pounded in her ears as she forced composure. "I'll expose you. The world will know who you are and what you do."

"Exposing us will only lead to your demise," the figure whispered, drawing closer. "Pledge yourself to the shadows, or be sacrificed like the rest."

With a swift movement, the figure lunged at her, but Mia reacted instinctively, ducking out of the way and launching herself from the branch in a roll, landing deftly on her feet. The cult members below turned their attention to the commotion, the chanting halting as confusion rippled through the crowd.

Seeing her chance, Mia dashed toward the altar, her heart pounding as she reached the bowl of dark liquid. "Stop!" she cried, adrenaline fueling her voice.

The leader, momentarily stunned, turned his gaze toward her. "Foolish girl! You cannot interfere!"

"I won't let you take another life!" Mia shouted, shoving the bowl over, sending the contents spilling across the altar and pooling on the ground. The crowd gasped, confusion turning to anger as the dark liquid seeped into the soil—a symbol of their power being desecrated.

As the cult members erupted in chaos, Peters burst onto the scene alongside a group of backup officers he had managed to ring in. "Mia!" he shouted, running toward her. "Get the girl!"

The chaos exploded into full motion as Peters tackled the cult leader, drawing the crowd further into disarray. Mia ran toward the girl, untangling the ropes that bound her as the rest of the cult members began to retreat in panic, their once ominous chanting now transformed into cries of fear.

"Come on, we need to get you out of here!" Mia urged, her hands working quickly to free the girl.

But as they stumbled back toward safety, a loud roar erupted from the cult leader, who had wrenched himself free from Peters' grip. In the chaos, his voice lifted above the fray, "You cannot escape the shadows! They are everywhere, watching, waiting!"

The remaining cult members swirled around him, forming a protective barrier, faces twisted with rage and desperation. Mia felt the weight of their malice bearing down upon her. Even as sirens wailed in the distance, she understood that the darkness within Ravenwood was far from extinguished—it was just getting started.

"Into the darkness?" she whispered, glancing at Peters as they pulled the girl to safety. "No, this is just the beginning. We've only scratched the surface."

And as the shadows closed in around them, Mia knew that she had taken a perilous step into a world of darkness that would demand everything from her if she was to combat the cult and its insidious grip on the town. The fight was only beginning, and she would need every ounce of strength to uncover the secrets shrouded in blood and darkness.

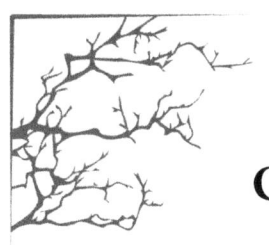

Chapter 17: The Revelation

The stillness of the night enveloped Ravenwood, the moonlight spilling silver over the landscape, casting long shadows that writhed like restless spirits. Mia stood in front of the abandoned church once more, her breath visible in the chilly air, a ghostly reminder of the tension building inside her. After weeks unearthing secrets buried deep in the town's history, she sensed that they were on the brink of a monumental breakthrough.

Tonight would bring the truth to light—or seal their fates in darkness.

Since their discovery of the cult's rituals in the church, Mia and Peters had gathered enough information to suspect a forthcoming ceremony. Whispers of a ritual aligned with the lunar calendar were woven into the cult's teachings, one that promised transformation and renewal through blood sacrifice.

They had spent countless hours identifying key members of the Cult of Shadows, gathering intel on their movements, and identifying potential participants. The culmination of their efforts had led them here, standing outside the church where the cult had made its home.

"Mia," Peters called, his voice barely above a whisper as they made their way through the creeping mist, "are you sure about this?"

Mia nodded, her resolve firmer than ever. "We have to put a stop to whatever is happening tonight. If they're planning to use Rebecca as a part of their ritual, we can't let that happen."

Together, they moved cautiously through the overgrown path leading to the back entrance. The air hummed with impending dread, each crackling twig or rustling leaf amplifying their anxiety. Finally, they reached the rear door, which swung open eerily, revealing the entrance to a chamber filled with flickering candles that cast eerie shadows on the walls.

Voices flowed softly from within, blending into an almost melodic hum, a chant resonating with an ancient rhythm Mia felt deep in her bones. The rituals she had unearthed were true; the cult was preparing for something significant.

"Stay close," she whispered to Peters, who nodded, his expression grave.

They slipped inside, pressing against the damp wall, peering into the dimly lit room where cloaked figures moved around a makeshift altar. The sight was almost surreal—a tableau of shadowy forms, each one marked by the same sigils Mia had seen in the journals.

At the center of the scene stood a man she recognized immediately: The Seer. He wore a hood that concealed his face, but even so, the air felt charged around him. He raised his arms, commanding the attention of the assembled members, their faces obscured by darkness yet alive with fervor.

"Tonight, we reclaim the essence of power!" he declared, his voice booming with authority that sent shivers down Mia's spine. "Tonight, we transcend our mortal chains, and the one chosen shall be reborn!"

Mia's pulse quickened. The words ignited a sense of urgency, and she scanned the room until her eyes fell on an object of horror: bound and kneeling before the altar was Rebecca Lane.

"No!" Peters hissed, his eyes wide with shock.

"Wait," Mia whispered urgently, pulling him back. They needed to act carefully. Storming in without a plan could spell disaster for Rebecca.

SECRETS CARVED IN BLOOD

The chanting grew louder, a feverish crescendo that echoed off the walls. Mia felt the weight of the moment pressing down on her. This was it—the culmination of everything she had uncovered. She needed to expose the truth behind this heinous act, but first, they had to free Rebecca.

Through the thrumming noise, she caught snippets of conversation. "We cannot hesitate! The time is now!" one of the cult members shouted, urgency lacing their tone.

Suddenly, The Seer raised a dagger, its blade glinting ominously in the candlelight. "With this blood, we renew our pact with the shadows!"

"Now!" Mia commanded, adrenaline surging as she and Peters stepped into the room, guns drawn. "Drop the dagger! Back away from her!"

The room fell into chaos as cult members turned their attention toward the intruders. The once hypnotic chanting shattered into shouts of confusion and fear.

"Get her out of here!" Peters yelled, opening fire on the ground near The Seer, who recoiled in surprise. The shot rang out, a deafening crack that echoed against the walls, and then chaos erupted.

"Intruders!" The Seer barked, anger twisting his features. "Seize them!"

Mia lunged forward, closing the distance between herself and Rebecca. "Hold on, I'm coming!" She aimed her weapon at a nearby figure, forcing them to back away as she knelt beside Rebecca, panic and relief flooding her.

Rebecca's eyes widened, full of terror but also recognition. "Mia...?"

"Shhh, I've got you," Mia whispered, expertly loosening the ropes binding Rebecca's wrists. "We're getting you out of here."

Cult members surged forward, shadows under the command of The Seer. Peters fired again, hitting one in the leg, but the chaos was overwhelming.

"Mia, we need a way out!" he yelled, his voice strained as he fended off the advancing figures.

"Through the side door!" Mia shouted, already ushering Rebecca to her feet. Adrenaline coursed through her, steadying her hands as she propelled Rebecca toward safety.

They dashed toward the exit, but before they could reach it, an imposing figure blocked their path. It was The Seer, his dagger raised, fury in his eyes. "You meddle in forces you cannot comprehend!"

Mia felt a rush of fear but pushed it aside. "We're not afraid of you!"

Peters moved beside her, firing another warning shot. "Get out of the way! This is your final chance!"

The Seer laughed darkly, lowering the dagger for a moment as he regarded them with disdain. "You think you can stop what has already been set into motion?"

Mia seized the moment. "This ends now!"

With one swift motion, she lunged forward, grappling the dagger from his hand, feeling the weight of the blade as their eyes locked. Time seemed to freeze, the world narrowing to the two of them, each breath filled with intensity. Then she delivered a swift kick to The Seer's knee, and he fell, off balance.

Peters assisted, forcing the cultists backward, creating a path for their escape. "This way! Now!"

They sprinted through the now chaotic space, the chants morphing into cries of disbelief and anger behind them.

Bursting into the night air, Mia felt the cool breeze wash over her as they raced across the yard. Heart pounding, she quickly glanced back to see The Seer scrambling to his feet, fury etched on his features as he shouted orders.

"Get to the car!" Peters yelled, panic driving his voice.

They reached the vehicle, and Mia fumbled with the keys, her hands trembling from adrenaline and fear. Finally, the engine roared to life, but she couldn't shake the feeling that this wasn't over. They weren't just escaping; they were igniting a war within the town's shadows.

As they sped away, Rebecca barely spoke, her expression a mixture of confusion and terror. Mia glanced over at her, their eyes meeting in a moment of understanding. "You're safe now. We'll figure this out together."

But as they drove toward the horizon, the weight of revelations loomed over them. The Cult of Shadows was not defeated; they were enraged, and Mia knew this was just the beginning of a battle that would pit them against dark forces they were only beginning to comprehend.

In the depths of the night, the whispers of the Cult chased them; shadows that would not fade easily—as long as their secrets remained buried deep within Ravenwood.

Chapter 18: Redemption's Price

The night sky loomed heavy over Ravenwood, the air thick with an unsettling tension that mirrored the turmoil brewing in Mia's heart. Having uncovered layers of deception and dark secrets, she found herself standing at the precipice of chaos, the weight of the investigation pressing down on her like a storm cloud threatening to burst. All the threads she had painstakingly unraveled now twisted and intertwined, leading her to an inevitable confrontation.

Mia stood outside the old church, the Cult of Shadows' meeting place, her breath misting in the cold air. She had set the trap, luring the cult members to gather under the guise of an important announcement. Tonight, she was determined to shine a light on the darkness they had hidden for too long.

Peters approached, his expression a mix of concern and resolve. "Are you sure about this? We don't know how they'll react—this could get dangerous."

Mia nodded, steeling her resolve. "I've seen what these people are capable of. We can't let them operate in the shadows any longer. If they want a confrontation, then we'll give them one."

As they moved inside, the flickering of candles casting elongated shadows across the walls added to the church's eerie atmosphere. Mia could hear the muted whispers of cult members gathering, their voices blending into a menacing hum that settled deep into her bones.

"Remember your plan," Peters reminded her, his voice low. "Stick to the script. We just need to gather evidence and get out."

She shot him a reassuring smile, but inside she felt a tumult of emotions—fear, anger, and an undeniable sense of duty. Each step toward the gathering felt like stepping into the mouth of a predator, but she couldn't turn back now. Not after everything she had seen, everything she had lost.

The main hall of the church was bustling with members, their dark robes swirling around them like cobwebs obscuring her view of the faces she now recognized. The Seer stood at the front, a figure cloaked in authority and menace, commanding the attention of the crowd with an air of cold confidence.

"Welcome, followers!" The Seer's voice resonated through the vaulted ceiling, echoing like a proclamation of doom. "Tonight, we gather to renew our pact with the shadows and embrace the potential that lies within the sacrifice."

Mia exchanged glances with Peters, tension hanging between them. They had to act now. Taking a deep breath, she stepped forward, her heart hammering in her chest.

"Enough!" Mia's voice cut through the murmur of the crowd, every eye turning toward her. "You don't need to do this. We know about your rituals, the blood shed in the name of your cult."

A ripple of confusion surged through the members, many stepping back as the reality of her presence sank in. The Seer's eyes narrowed on her, dark and calculating. "Detective Hart," he acknowledged, venom dripping from every syllable. "You've come to disrupt our gathering. But you underestimate the power of shadows."

"Power built on manipulation, fear, and sacrifice," Mia shot back, her voice steadier than she felt. "You prey on the vulnerable, masking your dark practices with delusions of grandeur."

The crowd shifted uneasily, uncertainty rippling through them. "There's nothing delusional about the truth we seek. It is you who is blind, Detective," The Seer replied, a twisted smile curling on his lips. "We are the true guardians of Ravenwood."

"Guardians?" Peters echoed, stepping beside Mia, his presence a solid anchor. "You're nothing but monsters hiding behind a façade. You think you can control death, but all you do is destroy lives."

The Seer's expression darkened. "You are playing a dangerous game, Detective. We have seen your struggles, your vulnerabilities. Each of your failures has been a thread in our tapestry—woven even now to bring about what must come next."

Mia felt a shiver run through her, fear spilling into her resolve. The shadows in the room thickened, the flickering candles igniting a tempest of chaos. But she knew this was a turning point, because the truth had always been her weapon. "What's coming next?" she demanded, stepping forward once again. "Tell me!"

A low murmur swept through the congregation, a collective shroud of silence enveloping their leader. The Seer raised a hand, and moments later, a figure emerged from the darkness—a girl, no older than twenty, eyes wide with terror, dragged roughly into the light.

"Stop!" Mia shouted, instinctively rushing forward. "You can't do this!"

The Seer laughed, a chilling sound that echoed through the church. "This girl is a chosen vessel. Her purity will ensure our ascendance—an offering that will transcend us to greatness. This is the price of redemption."

Heart pounding, Mia realized they had one chance to intervene. "You think sacrificing her will redeem any of you?" she countered, her voice trembling with fierce determination. "True redemption comes from righting wrongs, not inflicting them on others!"

The crowd wavered, doubt flickering in their eyes. It was a crack in their facade, and Mia pressed on. "You are not bound by shadows! You can choose to walk in the light and break free from the cycle of blood and sacrifice."

"For every one who leaves, a hundred will follow!" The Seer's voice thundered, anger rippling through him. The darkness pulsed, a tangible aura of menace that tightened around them.

Suddenly, the tension snapped. Peters moved to secure the girl, but chaos erupted. Shadows surged forward, members of the cult lunging at Mia and Peters with wild frenzy. The church erupted into a maelstrom of fists and cries as Mia fought her way through the conflict, reaching for the girl.

"Get out!" Peters shouted, his voice strained as he grappled with a cult member, desperately trying to protect both Mia and the captive girl.

In the midst of the chaos, Mia's eyes locked with the girl's, a silent plea for freedom. With a final surge of adrenaline, she grasped the girl's arm, pulling her close. "Run! This way!" Mia yelled, guiding her toward the exit.

As they broke through the back door, fresh air assaulted them, the sounds of the struggle fading into the night. Mia felt the cool wind wash over her, invigorating her as they stumbled into the clearing outside the church.

Breathless and shaking, Mia turned to the girl, locking eyes with her. "Are you okay?"

"I think so," she whispered, her face pale but resolute. "Thank you. I thought... I thought they were going to kill me."

"Not on my watch," Mia breathed, relief flooding through her. "We need to get you to safety. There will be more of them coming."

Suddenly, the sound of laughter echoed from the church, the voices of the cult members spilling out like a dark tide. The Seer's voice rose above the chaos, filled with a predatory threat. "You think you've won? The shadows will always find a way back!"

Peters rallied behind them, breathless and battered, but unwavering. "Let's go! We need to get to the car!"

Together, they sprinted through the underbrush, the shadows of the trees closing in around them. Mia felt the girl's hand gripped tightly in hers as they burst into the parking lot, adrenaline surging in a desperate bid for safety.

"Mia, hurry!" Peters called, already at the car, fumbling with the keys.

As they dove inside, the sense of urgency heightened. They could hear the cult members approaching, the flickering lanterns illuminating the path behind them.

"Drive! Go!" Mia urged Peters, while the girl huddled against the window, breathing heavily.

The engine roared to life, and they raced away, the darkness of the church receding behind them as they fled into the night. Mia's hands shook, not just from the adrenaline but from the weight of what had happened. They had uncovered the cult, but in doing so, they had stirred a dangerous beast.

"We need to tell the others," Peters said, determination etched on his face as he glanced back toward the road they had escaped. "We need to make sure they can't hurt anyone else."

Mia nodded, fear still coursing through her veins. She would not let another life be claimed by the shadows; the price of redemption would not be paid in blood.

As the lights of the town loomed closer, Mia steeled her resolve. They had exposed the darkness, but the battle was far from over. The shadows could not be vanquished so easily, and she was prepared to face whatever lay ahead to ensure that the truth would shine through, no matter the cost.

Chapter 19: The Last Stand

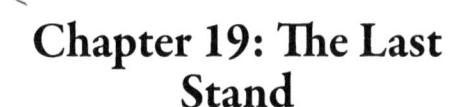

The moon hung high, a ghostly orb illuminating the clearing where the Cult of Shadows had chosen to carry out their final ritual. Mia Hart stood behind a cluster of trees, the air thick with tension, anticipation, and a primal fear that reverberated through the night. She could hear the murmurs of incantations wafting through the breeze, a haunting melody laced with urgency.

Beside her, Detective Peters crouched low, scanning the area with a flashlight, its beam flickering over the figures cloaked in dark robes gathered around an old stone altar. The cult members moved in synchronized rhythm, their hoods obscuring their faces, creating a tableau of shadowy figures framed against the flickering light of torches.

"Are we too late?" Peters whispered, anxiety lacing his voice.

Mia's heart pounded in her chest as she peered closer, locking her gaze onto the altar. Atop it lay a ceremonial dagger, gleaming in the moonlight, its blade stained with echoes of past bloodshed. And there, at the center of the gathering, stood The Seer—a tall figure who radiated authority, the leader whose very presence commanded the members' unwavering loyalty.

"We're not late," Mia replied, steeling herself. "We need to wait for the right moment. If they're performing some kind of sacrifice, we can't intervene now without jeopardizing the situation."

"But what if they're targeting someone? What if Rebecca's name is on their lips?" Peters countered, his brow furrowed with concern.

"We don't know if they've already taken her. We have to be precise." Mia's resolve hardened. "We need to gather evidence and stop this for good."

As the chanting grew louder, echoing through the trees like an incantation from the depths of despair, Mia's mind raced with thoughts of Rebecca, of Lila, of all the lives the cult had touched—ruined. The stakes had never felt higher.

Suddenly, there was a shift in the air, the energy in the clearing snapping like a live wire. The Seer raised his hands, commanding silence, and all eyes turned toward him. "Tonight, we embrace the shadows!" he proclaimed, his voice a dark crescendo that resonated through the forest. "Tonight, we break the chains of our earthly confines. Let the blood of the unworthy flow and grant us the power we seek!"

Mia's gut tightened. They had to act. "We need backup," she murmured to Peters, pulling out her phone. She quickly dialed dispatch, her fingers trembling as she relayed their location. "We need immediate assistance. There's a cult performing a ritual at Miller's Park. It's urgent!"

As she ended the call, the atmosphere thickened, and the torchlight flickered ominously. The Seer stepped closer to the altar, and Mia could see the gleaming edge of the dagger in his hand. "Bring forth the sacrifice!" he boomed.

Mia's breath hitched as a figure was pushed to the front of the group, struggling against the grip of two members. It was Lila. Fear paralyzed Mia as she watched her friend, her face pale and eyes wide with terror.

"No!" Mia shouted, rushing forward before she could fully process the consequences. "Stop!"

The cultists turned, shock rippling through their ranks as Mia emerged from the shadows, Peters at her side. "Get away from her!" she commanded, her voice steady despite the chaos unfolding in her mind.

"Mia?" Lila's voice trembled, desperate and filled with disbelief.

The Seer's eyes narrowed, his dismissive smile cutting through the dark. "Another foolish soul comes to disrupt the sacred rites. You have no power here, Detective."

"I have the power to end this," Mia shot back, her heart racing with a mix of fury and determination. "You're not going to sacrifice anyone else tonight."

A flicker of amusement crossed The Seer's face. "You think you can stop destiny? Blood will be spilled, and tonight shall bring forth a new era."

"Not on my watch." Mia glanced at Peters, who was already positioned to watch her back.

As the cult members began to move, a ripple of uncertainty spread among them, their faces shrouded in darkness. She knew they had to act swiftly. "We can't let this go on!"

In that moment, Peters surged forward, pushing against the nearest cultist. Chaos erupted; cultists shouted, confusion spreading as they turned on each other. "Mia! Get Lila out of here!" he yelled.

With adrenaline surging, Mia dashed to Lila, reaching her just as the torches began to flicker dangerously, the flames leaping higher. "I got you," Mia whispered, scooping Lila into her arms and pulling her away from the altar.

But resistance was futile. The Seer raised the dagger, his expression twisted with rage. "Seize her!"

As the cultists lunged forward, Mia's mind raced. She pulled Lila closer and dove to the side, feeling the rush of air as its path shifted, narrowly avoiding the clutches of a robed figure. They turned, and the dagger glinted in the moonlight, the promise of darkness just a breath away.

"Get down!" Peters shouted, and in an instant, he tackled one of the cultists away from the altar, but more were closing in.

Mia barely registered what happened next. The world became a blur of frantic movement, shouts, and the booming laughter of The Seer, who directed his followers with a ferocity that sent chills down her spine. As the chaos unfolded, she caught a glimpse of the knives and torches, countless threats aimed at her and Peters.

"We have to get them to surrender!" Mia yelled, pulling out her gun, the familiar weight grounding her focus.

"You think you can stop this?" The Seer taunted, his voice dripping with contempt. "Your feeble attempts to undermine the shadows will only strengthen our purpose!"

"Enough!" Mia shot back, raising her weapon. "You need to surrender. It's over."

In that instance, a cacophony erupted, shouts merging into a tidal wave of noise. Peters, outnumbered, grappled with the nearest cultist, but was pulled back as a second figure lunged toward Mia.

She ducked, narrowly avoiding grasping hands, and aimed at the desperate figure. "Don't make me use this!" she warned, her voice steady, unwavering.

The structure of the cult began to collapse under the chaotic struggle, a sense of discordant energy swirling in the air. Lila clutched Mia's arm, fear evident in her eyes. "We have to get out of here!"

Just then, the sound of sirens pierced through the night, a beacon of hope. "Backup's here!" Peters yelled, pushing back another cult member. "We need to hold them off until they arrive!"

Mia felt a surge of bravery, but it was quickly dampened by fear as more cultists pressed in from all sides. "FBI! Everyone freeze! This is your last warning!" The voice came from the treeline as federal agents burst into the clearing, armed and ready, their badges glinting in the pale light.

As the agents moved in, The Seer attempted to rally his followers, cutting through the fray with chilling authority. "Do not let them take what belongs to us! Stand firm!"

But gradually, the mix of confusion and fear took hold, the cultists realizing they were about to be outmatched. The agents closed in, guns drawn, shouting commands, and one by one, the cult members began to hesitate, glancing at each other as uncertainty rippled through their ranks.

"Now!" Mia shouted, her heart pounding as she and Peters pushed forward, aiming to intercept The Seer before he could escape. "Get Lila to safety!"

Peters nodded, moving to protect Lila as she stumbled close to him, fear still clouding her eyes. With her backup arrived, Mia felt an adrenaline rush, firing directly at the altar, aiming to dismantle the remnants of the cult's power with every ounce of her will.

"You cannot escape your fate!" The Seer screamed, brandishing the dagger, a last act of defiance. But the agents surrounded him, their weapons trained and unwavering.

"Put down the weapon!" an agent barked, approaching with authority.

Realizing the end was near, The Seer hesitated, confusion spread across his face, mingling with rage. "You don't know what you're doing!"

But Mia knew exactly what she was doing. "You're done!" she shouted, ready to see justice served.

In a final act of desperation, the cult leader raised the dagger high, but it was too late. The agents surged forward, disarming him with practiced ease, the dagger clattering to the ground, echoing like a clap of thunder in the chaos.

As the cult members began to surrender, the oppressive weight of fear began to lift. The air grew lighter, the whispers of the shadows waning as the night turned into dawn, revealing slivers of light breaking through the trees, illuminating the clearing one last time.

Mia took a deep breath, her heart racing, the triumph of survival and the grief for the fallen mingling in her chest. They had won this battle, but they couldn't forget the scars it left behind. She turned to Lila, who was still trembling but alive, and relief washed over her like a gentle tide.

"Let's get you out of here," Mia said softly, leading Lila toward the agents, who were handcuffing the remaining cult members.

As they walked away from the remnants of the ritual, the dawn breaking behind them, Mia realized their fight might be over for now, but the shadows that had plagued Ravenwood would not be forgotten. Their scars would remain, whispering for justice, and it would be her job to ensure that the echoes of the Cult of Shadows faded into mere history, banished to the depths from which they had risen.

With every footstep toward safety, aware of the lives shattered but resolute for those who could be saved, Mia felt the fire of determination flare within her. This was not the end—merely the last stand against the looming darkness, and she would ensure that it wasn't in vain.

Chapter 20: Secrets Laid to Rest

The sun hung low in the sky, casting a golden hue over Ravenwood as Mia stood on the precipice of what had become a battleground of truths. Today marked a culmination of nights and days spent unraveling the tangled web of darkness that had enveloped her town, a battle against secrets that sought to remain buried.

The local park was eerily quiet, the air thick with anticipation. In the distance, a crowd began to gather, drawn by whispers of a community meeting called to address the recent tragedies. Mia, flanked by Peters and a handful of officers, felt the weight of responsibility pressing against her chest. She was about to expose the truth—everything she had discovered about the Cult of Shadows, about Rebecca Lane, and about the hidden faces that lurked in the wings of silence.

"Are you ready?" Peters asked quietly, studying her closely.

Mia nodded, pushing back the flicker of doubt that threatened her resolve. "Let's do this."

As they approached the makeshift podium, she noticed familiar faces among the crowd, some filled with anxiety, others with suspicion. The fabric of their community had been frayed, and Mia understood the task ahead was not merely to inform but to heal.

"Thank you all for coming," Mia began, her voice steady yet filled with the gravity of the moment. "It's time we faced the truth. A darkness has crept into our town, hidden among us, manipulating lives and instilling fear."

Murmurs rippled through the crowd. She took a breath, grounding herself. "Rebecca Lane's death was not random. She fell victim to a cult operating discreetly within Ravenwood—the Cult of Shadows."

A collective gasp echoed, disbelief hanging in the air. She pressed on. "For years, this group has thrived on secrecy, drawing in vulnerable individuals, holding rituals that could only serve their insidious agenda. Rebecca was trying to escape her past, and in that struggle, she became entangled in theirs."

Faces shifted from shock to anger, and Mia could see the battle for understanding beginning to unfurl. "Many of you may have seen their gatherings. You may have witnessed their members at the edges of this community. But it's important to know that you are not alone. We will not let this continue unchecked."

Peters stepped forward, holding a stack of evidence—photos, journals, and witness statements that corroborated Mia's points. "We have compiled everything we found, and we're working to ensure that these individuals face justice. But we need your help. If you've seen something unusual, say something."

A voice rose from the crowd, a woman Mia recognized as Mrs. Jenkins. "How do we know who's involved? How can we trust that this is really happening?"

Mia met her gaze, fierce and unwavering. "I know this is frightening. The truth is that those involved wear faces you may recognize. They blend in. But we will be vigilant. We plan to increase patrols and keep an eye on any suspicious activities. Together, we can protect our town."

Several people began to murmur in agreement, emboldened by her words. "Yes!" a voice shouted from the back. "We need to take our town back!"

Mia felt a surge of hope, but fear still clung to her like a shroud. "If any of you have information or feel threatened, please reach out to us immediately. We have a task force ready and willing to assist."

Another voice rang out. "What about the ones who are already involved? What if they retaliate?"

Mia steeled herself. "We will do everything in our power to protect you. But I need you to stand with us. Silence has kept this cult alive, and only by breaking that silence can we reclaim our community."

As she spoke, she felt the energy shift. People began to rally, their fear transmuting into determination. She saw Lila in the crowd, eyes wide but filled with resolve, nodding as if she understood the power of solidarity.

The sun dipped lower, and as shadows stretched longer, Mia realized they were wrestling not just with the demons of this cult but with their own past failures to see the signs. Tonight, they would face those shadows together.

"Let's stand united!" Peters raised his voice, galvanizing the crowd. "Let's protect our town!"

Cheers erupted, a cacophony of voices rising in unison. Mia felt a warmth spreading through her chest, a fierce hope igniting in the hearts of those gathered. They would not allow darkness to define them.

As the meeting began to wind down, people lingered, discussing the next steps they could take. Mia felt weary yet invigorated, aware that the real work was just beginning. Together, they would confront the past, one step at a time.

Suddenly, a thought crossed her mind—a reflection of everything she had been through, everything she had lost and gained. The case had changed her, taught her lessons about trust, resilience, and the strength of community.

As the last rays of sunlight faded, Mia felt a sense of peace descend. Secrets had been laid bare, and though scars remained, they would heal. Ravenwood was not just a town; it was a living entity, filled with stories woven together by a history that could no longer be ignored.

She turned to Peters, sharing a small smile. "We did it."

"Yeah," he replied, his eyes gleaming with pride and relief. "And we're just getting started."

As night enveloped the town, a sense of purpose settled over them. Together, they would rebuild, giving voice to those silenced by darkness. Secrets had been laid to rest, but from the ashes of those secrets, a new beginning emerged. And with it, a fierce resolve to ensure that Ravenwood would never again become a haven for shadows.

Don't miss out!

Visit the website below and you can sign up to receive emails whenever Walter Moon publishes a new book. There's no charge and no obligation.

https://books2read.com/r/B-A-AXVLC-PVOIF

BOOKS 2 READ

Connecting independent readers to independent writers.